A Stranger Comes to Town

A Stranger Comes to Town

Lynne Sharon Schwartz

A Stranger Comes to Town
Lynne Sharon Schwartz

FICTION
ISBN   978-1-958094-63-1

Book Design ~ EK LARKEN
Cover Design ~ DAVIN MALASARN
Cover Image ~ LUCY ORLOSKI
   ["back bay at night" by l . e . o is licensed under CC BY 2.0.]
Author Photo ~ SUSYE GREENWOOD

EastOver Press encourages the use of our publications in
educational settings. For questions about educational discounts,
contact us online: www.EastOverPress.com or
info@EastOverPress.com.

PUBLISHED IN THE UNITED STATES OF AMERICA BY

EastOver Press
Rochester, Massachusetts
www.EastOverPress.com

All great literature is one of two stories:
a man goes on a journey
or a stranger comes to town.

— Leo Tolstoi

AT THE MOMENT I CAN'T OFFER A THOROUGH introduction. The mirror shows that I'm a white male, late thirties, fairly good-looking in an unremarkable way, nice cheekbones, hair light brown, eyes grey, face that improves considerably if I smile, which I'm finding it hard to do just now. I'm living in a brownstone in Manhattan, where I go by the name Joe, innocuous enough. Most of my housemates call me Dad or Daddy. The name Joe Marzino was found in my wallet, which was found in the back pocket of my shorts. My wallet? So I'm told, but it's not inconceivable that it's someone else's wallet placed in my pocket for an unknown and not benign reason, while I lay unconscious on the sidewalk a block away from New York's Central Park. That is the story I've been told.

I don't remember seeing this house before the afternoon when I was brought here by the woman claiming to be my wife, with whom I now share a bed. She assures me I'm the father of three children, our children, presentable, unobjectionable children, I thought when I first saw them. They make a pleasant family for someone in need of one. Now after a couple of weeks of getting to know them, I've grown quite fond of them, mine or not. I love them, without remembering all the years when they came to be who they are. I miss those. But I should feel lucky—it could have been worse had some other woman come to the hospital to claim me—or no woman at all—after what I'm told was an accident involving a bicycle that knocked me to the ground and obliterated my memory, which might or might not return, all or part of it.

The first thing I remember of my present life is lying flat on my back with a woman leaning over me repeating, "Name? Name? Tell me your name, please?"

I couldn't. I had no name, I had nothing except the clothes on my back and a throbbing pain in my left ankle.

"Name?" she urged.

Her face hovered over me, dark, young, tense. Maybe a trifle impatient. She wore large purplish glasses in which I could see my face. An anxious face, baffled, streaked with sweat and dirt …

She said, "I'm an EMT, and you're in an ambulance on the way to the hospital. I have your wallet right here. If you have no objections, I'll find some ID in there. Do I have your permission?"

I nodded.

"Your name is Joe Marzino," she said. "So, Joe, how do you feel? Does it hurt anywhere?"

I sent my mind wandering along my body and rubbed my eyes as if that would help. "My ankle. The left."

"Yes, there's a bad bruise there. We'll have it x-rayed. Anywhere else? No? You were knocked down by a bicycle on Columbus Avenue. Maybe you were jogging, you've got on sneakers and shorts, and you're kind of sweaty. Are you a jogger? Can you remember what happened?" I recognized the lilting accent. Jamaica.

I shook my head.

"What's the last thing you remember?"

I thought for a while. "Nothing." I felt stupid, embarrassed, like a child in school who's called on and can't answer the teacher's question. How come I recognize a Jamaican accent when I didn't recognize my own name?

"Okay, don't worry. You'll be fine soon. Are you married? We'd like to call your wife or your next of kin."

I shrugged.

"I have your phone here, and there's a number for home. We'll try that."

A scrim of drowsiness fell on the scene. When I woke, I was being wheeled through beige-colored corridors, lots of doors, large ugly abstract paintings on the walls. Clearly a hospital. Knowing something, anything at all, was a relief. I was wheeled into a small room where a cluster of men and women in grape-green outfits with name tags was leaning over me, poking and prodding. Name tags are a good idea, maybe we should all wear them, in case of situations like mine. A looming monitor displayed green lines wiggling about on a black background. Someone attached an IV to the back of my hand. I knew what an IV was. They asked many questions, but I didn't know the answers to most of them, not my address or what I did for a living. I did know the name of the president—Obama—but not the year. They asked my address, but I couldn't answer. They read out an address they claimed was mine, but it meant nothing to me.

"Do you know Central Park? You were found a block from the park. Do you go jogging there?"

After they got no answers, I was wheeled into an elevator and then to a double room. It must have been a high floor—out the window, way down below, was the park, its twining paths suggesting a child's board game. A nurse, not the one from the ambulance, blonde, older, with a careworn face, asked me what I saw, and I said Central Park: rowboats on a lake, a few horses and carriages for the tourists. She seemed pleased—this time I was a clever lad who had answered correctly.

"I'm going to tell you a few facts about yourself, and I'll come back in a little while and see what you remember, okay?" she said. "Your name is Joe Marzino, you're thirty-seven years old, you live on West 84th Street, you work on West 57th Street, from the photos on your phone it looks like you have children … two? Three?" she asked. "You're not an organ donor, you have a driver's license, a library card and several credit cards, you're in the Road Runners club and in Actors' Equity …"

"How do you know so much about me?"

She waved the wallet at me. "It's all in here, Joe, this is your life. You have fifty-six dollars in your wallet. All of that and your keys will be returned to you when you're discharged."

Keys. To what? "When will I be discharged?" When can I go home, is what I wanted to ask, but the word "home" didn't suggest anything specific.

"Whenever the doctors say you're ready. We'll be doing x-rays to see if you need surgery on that ankle. And an MRI pretty soon. Try to be patient. By the way, you look familiar. Were you in the emergency room a couple of weeks ago with a teenaged boy?"

"I don't know. What was wrong with him?"

"It wasn't serious. He slipped playing soccer at school and hit his head, but he only needed a few staples. No internal bleeding."

"Staples?"

"Yes, we use them often now instead of stitches."

ANY DOCTOR WILL TELL YOU THAT THE incidence of amnesia in books and movies is far greater than it is in actual life. Rarely do people get hit on the head or fall off a ladder and get back on their feet muttering, Who am I? Where am I? This, the medical profession maintains, is the stuff of fiction. "Real, diagnosable amnesia," the novelist Jonathan Lethem writes in an anthology of stories on the subject, "people getting knocked on the head and forgetting their names—is mostly just a rumor in the world. It's a rare condition, and usually a brief one. In books and movies, though, versions of amnesia lurk everywhere … Amnesiacs might not much exist, but amnesiac characters stumble everywhere through comic books, movies, and our dreams. We've all met them and been them." In my case, his final words can be taken literally.

There are many kinds of amnesia, as anyone can find through a quick Google search, but the *Who am I? Where am I?* kind that I have, retrograde amnesia, doesn't prevent you from doing Google searches, or driving a car, or remembering how to mix a Martini (or in my case, as I would soon find out, memorizing a new script). Yet medical websites agree that "although TV shows and movies portray people with amnesia losing their entire identities, that only happens in rare psychiatric conditions … Fortunately, amnesia usually isn't that severe in real life." How fortunate I am, the following will reveal.

Why is amnesia such a favorite theme? For one thing, it offers a character who is a blank slate, although amnesiacs are said to keep their customary "personalities." (An oddness in itself, but more on that later.) We, the reader or movie-goer, ideally in the patient, accepting state of "negative capability" (I remember the phrase but not the source) wonder along with the afflicted character, what will be written on this slate? Is he or she a hero, a saint, an ordinary person? Not likely. Something has happened to bring on the condition—which will be revealed to us in good time—and the condition itself will generate more events. Mistakes, misfortunes, even tragedy, toxic secrets from the past—anything can happen, or may have happened.

In my case, I've been absorbed into a life. And there's ample proof that it is indeed my life, though I sometimes have trouble believing it. It's not so bad to be taken into a life. In an old movie starring Jim Carrey, the hero is washed up on the shore of a California town not knowing who he is, and is mistaken for a long-lost survivor of the war in Vietnam. He finds a loving father, a fiancée who had lost all hope of his return, and a ready-made business opportunity running the family movie theater. It all comes crashing down, of course, when he remembers his true identity—he is not as lucky as I, but that's beside the point. All ends well. (Yes, I do remember books and movies, and the multiplication tables and the conjugations of French verbs, just nothing I could call personal, my past.)

I've spent some time this last week or so watching old films about amnesia—research, I call it. In another film with a less happy outcome, the woman who claims to be the amnesiac's wife is an impostor who ends up torturing him. I turned it off at that point; I've never cared for horror movies, or I should say that right now I don't. I can't vouch for my past tastes. In any case I doubt I'll be mistreated here—so far my wife seems well-intentioned, even affectionate.

What would I have done had my "wife" not appeared? Most likely I would have gone to the address in the wallet, or been taken there, and found her and "our" children, so it would have turned out the same. On the other hand, if a stranger's wallet was substituted for my own for reasons that demand investigation, I might have been in danger. I don't know why anyone would have done that: I don't know if I am wealthy or involved in criminal activity or a secret agent. So I am fortunate, given the circumstances. If no other clues or memories turn up, it's best to assume that my "wife" is my wife and "our" children are our children—healthy, well brought up children; I'm grateful for my comfortable situation. It might have been far worse. It might have been a pallet and blanket under a viaduct. (These days when broken-down men or women ask me for money on the street, I always give.) Best to assume that whatever my past, in this case the world has treated me kindly. I do my best to play the role that has been thrust on me.

THE NURSE TURNED AT THE SOUND OF footsteps outside the curtain around my bed. "It looks like you have a visitor."

A tall woman with reddish hair piled messily but attractively on her head peeked through the curtain then rushed to my bed, bent down and hugged me.

"Joe, oh Joe. I was frantic when they called. Even though ... I dashed here from work. Luckily Vince was able to pick up Luz. Joe, baby, what happened? How are you?"

She was a beautiful woman, even without make-up and dressed in an old tee shirt and jeans. There was a name for that kind of hair ... an unusual color, auburn, yes, and looked natural—how did I know that? Was I a hairdresser? She had olive skin and extraordinary blue-green eyes with long lashes. Full lips and flushed cheeks. I stared. She looked like a woman who knew exactly who she was. Nothing vague or erased by memory here. If she were truly my wife, she would recall my every misstep.

"Joe, what's the matter?" She drew back.

"Your wife has come to see you, Mr. Marzino," the nurse said. She took the woman out past the curtain, where I heard them whispering. When they returned the nurse said, "I'll be back in a few moments to ask you some questions about what I told you, remember?"

"Joe," the beautiful woman said. "Joe, don't you know me? What's wrong? She said you hit your head. I thought it was just your ankle."

"I'm so sorry," I said. "It's good of you to come. But I … I can't remember anything. I don't even know your name. I'm awfully sorry." How could I be sure she was my wife? But I didn't want to be rude, in case she was telling the truth.

"Norah," she said and started to cry. "We've been married over fifteen years. Don't you remember?"

I shook my head, and she cried some more.

"Have a seat." I motioned to the bed and handed her some tissues from the box on the bedside table. "I'm sorry. Are you really my wife?"

"Why would I pretend? Don't you remember the children?"

When I shook my head again she bent her head and wept. "We have three children. Vincent is almost sixteen. Kevin is nine. And Luz is just four and a half. Does that remind you?"

"No."

She began giving me details—our kids, our house. With every detail I struggled to remember, but nothing came. Just a dark screen, as when a movie is over. Not even the credits. Nothing except my ankle, which was throbbing painfully. Her recitation of facts was more than I could cope with, so I closed my eyes and wished I could close my ears as well.

When she saw I was no longer listening, she simply sat on the bed holding my hand.

"I think I've been here before," I said, to ease her suffering in some small way. "Did I take a boy here with a head injury?"

"Oh, great!" she cried. "So you do remember something! I bet it will all come back soon. That was Vince; he hit his head playing soccer, and you raced to the hospital to be with him—I was at work. It was nothing much, thank goodness. He's fine now."

"I don't remember," I said. "The nurse told me. She remembered me." It was too bad to squash her relief, but I shouldn't offer false hope. Still, this was evidence that I was who she said I was, her husband and this soccer player's father. Unless another boy was injured, a boy with a father who resembled me. Or is that too crazy? Did I have a twin? A cousin? Or could this be part of the plot the nurse was in on?

The nurse returned with a pitcher of water and plastic cups and questioned me about the facts she gave me a while ago. I had to assume they were facts, unless I was trapped in a spy story. I remembered everything she'd said, my name, my age, the three children (well, Norah had just told me that), the Road Runners Club, everything. I didn't get the address exactly right but close enough to satisfy her. The Actors' Equity membership puzzled me.

"That's excellent," said the nurse. "A very good sign. So you're able to form new memories post-accident. You don't have anterograde amnesia." And she launched into some technical jargon about various types of amnesia; apparently mine wasn't the worst. The other kind meant I wouldn't be able to remember anything that happened after the accident. So you might lose your past or lose your future. A throw of the dice. I might recover my past in time or might not. There are more types of amnesia and more causes than I'd ever imagined, not that I had ever devoted much imagination to the subject, at least as far as I could recall. But of course I could recall nothing. Over the last couple of weeks I've learned a great deal, all of which I recall more clearly than I might wish. Not to mention the films and books based on the subject. But I'm getting ahead of myself.

In the hospital, I was suspicious of everything around me. I can't say whether I'm suspicious by nature or whether this was a result of my situation, or the accident. I might have been taken prisoner as part of some sinister plot and given a drug that erased my past. Maybe I'd watched too many crime stories on TV. How could I be sure that the woman, Norah, wasn't part of the plot? In movies people were drugged and hypnotized and made to carry out nefarious deeds they would never ordinarily do. *The Manchurian Candidate.* Strange to say, I remembered that well. Both versions, the old and the new. There might be other surprise memories of that nature. Well, in any event I wasn't about to obey any orders. I'd get my throbbing ankle taken care of and then get out of here.

But where could I go? Wherever the woman took me. To the address the nurse had read on the card in my wallet, most likely.

THE DAYS BLURRED, PUNCTUATED BY VISITS from neurologists who interrogated me, repeating themselves comically ad nauseam, giving me the same inane tests, could I touch my nose with a finger, could I roll my eyes. I obviously wasn't a doctor, or all this might have meant something to me. Anyhow, I must have passed everything because after a few days and a couple of MRIs, secluded in the sleek white coffin while hammers pounded in my ears, I was scheduled to be released.

Norah had tried to prepare me for my "homecoming" by giving me brief character sketches of the kids so I could act like their father. Otherwise they'd be upset, she said.

I objected. "If they're smart kids they'll know right away that something's wrong. I can't just put on an act," I said.

At that she laughed.

"What's so funny?"

"You're an actor, Joe. That's your profession. If you can act like a private detective, you can certainly act like a father."

"An actor. What kind of actor?"

"I just told you. On TV. You play a private eye, a tough guy in a weekly series. You solve cases the police can't manage. You push people around. You go into rough neighborhoods with your hand on your gun." She seemed to find this amusing.

"Oh, Christ. Is that how I am at home?"

"No, no, you're rather easygoing. Most of the time. Though lately—"

"Lately what?"

"Never mind. There'll be time for that. I'm glad you've forgotten."

Norah came to fetch me, like a pet left in the animal

hospital. Did we have a pet? I hoped not. Greeting the children would be bad enough without some cat slinking around my legs or a big dog leaping all over me. Or perhaps he wouldn't recognize me if this was not truly my home—that might be the test. In movies pets are very sure of whom they know and who are the strangers or impostors.

Stepping out into the sunshine onto a street with tall buildings, I hadn't the slightest idea where I was. Nothing looked familiar except the tall buildings I could see in the distance as we waited on the corner for a taxi.

"Did I grow up around here?" I asked Norah.

"Not far, on Riverside Drive. When you were a small child, you loved looking out your window at the river and the ships, your mother told me."

At the word "mother," a new set of questions unreeled in my head, like a dropped ball of yarn gone wild. Of course I must have, or have had, a mother. I must find out who and where she was, if she was still living. Why not? She couldn't be much more than sixty or so. And there'd have to be a father too. Sisters, brothers? Did they know about my accident, and were they likely to turn up? I must be prepared—it would be unforgivable not to recognize them. I'd ask Norah later, after we'd gotten over the hurdle of meeting the children.

I didn't tell her about the image in my head of the ships surrounded by ice floes in the frozen river. I didn't want to raise her hopes. I didn't want to talk at all. But she kept chattering about how thrilled the kids would be to see me.

In the taxi she warned me again. "Don't tell them right away about the … the memory loss," she urged. She had trouble bringing out the word. She wouldn't say amnesia. "It's too upsetting, at least so soon. Vince is old enough to deal with it, but the younger ones would be too disturbed if you acted like a stranger. They'd wonder if you're still their father."

As I wondered myself.

Vince, the oldest, she reminded me, was almost sixteen, a sophomore in high school. He played baseball and soccer and listened to heavy metal and was in the chess club. Despite the chess, he was outgoing and texted for hours with his friends. She spoke as if submitting an application; on the basis of those few facts did I wish to accept the role of father?

"So anyway can you just … act, you know, as if you know they're your kids?"

Kevin, who was nine, was quieter, more studious, a reader, had only a couple of close friends. He took clarinet lessons and was in the school band. He also played third base in Little League. I coached Little League on and off, she said, but with my injured ankle I wouldn't have to face that for a while. As I tried to absorb the facts—like preparing for an exam—I wished she would give me similar facts about myself: how had I become an actor, the most far-fetched profession I could imagine. It required remembering pages and pages of scripts when I couldn't remember who I was. What were my parents like, were we close or distant? Was I a rich kid, a poor kid, what was I interested in, what were my opinions, my tastes in music or books, friends? What were hers, for that matter? Who was she? Temperament? If she could sum up the kids so easily, perhaps she would do the same for me. I'd ask her, later. What kind of husband was I? Were we happy together? Did we have sex a lot? I started having a fantasy about being in bed with her but cut it short; this wasn't the moment.

She chattered on like a TV host on a game show

introducing the contestants. Luz, the youngest, was four and a half, very bright, already able to read, and went to a preschool program in the neighborhood. In the fall she would start kindergarten. Oh, and she was adopted. At birth.

"How come?"

"Kevin's was a very difficult birth, there were problems, and I was advised not to get pregnant again. But I wanted a girl so badly. So … She's crazy about you. Daddy's little girl."

I thought of the curly-haired blonde types I'd seen on TV and hoped she was nothing like that.

"Okay, I'll try to act like I'm their father. It sounds like I have plenty of experience. But don't be surprised if they don't fall for it."

The kids—my kids, our kids—met me at the door. Dad's back with only a sprained ankle, how lucky! Luz leaped into my arms, I had to catch her mid-air and dropped the cane I'd been given, while Vince took the overnight bag from Norah. Hugs all around—we were an affectionate family, evidently. Even Kevin, small and wiry, with Norah's coloring plus freckles and pale green eyes, was not too big to hug me around the chest. I lifted him and exclaimed at how heavy he'd grown. They seemed dismayed by the cane. "Daddy, will you have that forever now?" Luz asked, and I said no, sweetie, only for a few weeks until my ankle heals. I didn't know where that "sweetie" came from. The depths of memory, like muscle memory. Her small body was warm as I held her in my arms. She was nothing like the TV kids I'd imagined. Her skin was coppery, and she had straight shiny black hair cut short like a Beatle. A remarkably beautiful child with large, intense black eyes.

Vince looked like me, I could see right away, a strong

build. Athletic. I could feel the energy when he hugged me. His chiseled face, even features like mine, already had the inklings of a beard—I wondered if he shaved. It must be my job to teach him to shave. Had my father taught me? I felt my face. A few days growth from the hospital.

After I unpacked the overnight bag Norah had brought me, I lay down in our bedroom, a large airy room with a big double bed. Kevin and Luz wanted to climb on me, but Norah said they must let me rest until dinner. Dinner was an Italian dish with pesto and sausages, one of my favorites, she said. It was very good, though I couldn't say I liked it better than anything else. I didn't remember food except for the hospital food, which was food only in the most minimal sense. The kids' questions were mostly about the hospital, which I had no trouble answering. The tougher questions were yet to come.

"This is delicious. Do you do all the cooking?" I asked Norah.

"You know I do," she said, giving me a warning look. "Except for your specialties. Your meat loaf, for instance."

"I can make pretty good hot dogs and beans," said Vince.

"I made Valentine's Day cookies with Mommy," Luz said. "They were red and white."

"I remember," I lied. "They were awesome."

"You ate three," she said.

RIGHT AFTER THAT FIRST DINNER AT HOME I felt something gnawing at me, something other than my general unease and fear about the future. In addition to my past, something of another order entirely was missing, something specific that I needed.

Just as the boys got up and began clearing the table, it struck me. "Where are my cigarettes?"

"Joe!" Norah dropped the dish she was holding, like a shocked character in a sitcom. It didn't break. "You stopped. About a year and a half ago. Don't you remember?"

I couldn't have stopped. I could feel the itch in my throat and lungs. I remembered so vividly how it felt to light up and hold it between my fingers. My most tangible memory so far.

I shook my head. "Not really."

"We nagged you so much that you said you'd stop just to shut us up," said Kevin. "How could you forget that?"

"Well, I need them now. Look, I'm still a bit mixed up after the accident, the hospital, and all. I'll just dash out and get a pack. I can help you load the dishwasher first, though. I'm not that desperate."

"It's okay, I have plenty of help," said Norah. "It's your first night home."

"Fine." I went to look for my jacket. It was April, I'd seen on the wall calendar, and warmish. In the closet near the front door, crammed with coats and jackets, I found a navy windbreaker that must be mine. It looked too big for Vince, who was almost as tall as I was but not as broad. In one pocket was a crumpled handkerchief and some change. It was comforting to recognize the coins, quarters, dimes, nickels. I went upstairs to get my wallet with the fifty-six dollars. I remembered that.

"Which is the nearest place, I forget. Still a bit out of it," I felt the stupid grin on my face. It was pointless to try to hide my amnesia. They appeared to be bright kids; they'd catch on. Even if they weren't bright, they'd catch on.

"Down the block and across Columbus," said Vince crossly. "Shit, you go there every day for a paper. Forget it, I'll go."

"They won't sell to you, you're too young." It was curious, the little things I remembered— auburn hair, a Jamaican accent, and the legal age for buying cigarettes.

"You always send me when you run out. Amit knows me. Maybe you should rest up. Did you hit your head or something?"

"Actually I did. I have some slight memory loss."

I was relieved that Norah was not the kind of wife who stepped in to edit. So much for hiding my state.

"No, Vince, you finish with the dishes," said Norah. "Luz can go."

"Like in *The Bourne Identity*," Kevin said. "Remember? He doesn't even know who he is. And everyone wants to kill him."

"I don't think I saw that. But I doubt if anyone wants to kill me."

"We watched it together on TV," said Vince. "Remember he …"

"I guess I don't. But I remember other movies," I said defensively.

"Yeah, like what?"

"*The Manchurian Candidate*," I said. Vince and Kevin looked at each other and shrugged.

"*The Wizard of Oz*."

They snorted. "Yeah, just click your heels together and you'll be back home," said Vince.

"That's enough," Norah put in. "Luz, do you want to take a little walk with Daddy before your bath? Can you show him where Amit's is?"

She leaped from her seat and ran over to me at the door. "I saw *The Wizard of Oz*. Those monkeys were scary."

"You cried and we had to take you home. What do you mean by slight memory loss?" Kevin's voice caught in alarm. "Do you still know who we are?"

"Of course I do. It'll pass in a few days. Nothing to worry about."

After a brief but weighty silence, Norah said, "Remember to hold Daddy's hand when you cross the big street."

"Yes," Vince added, "or you'll lose him."

"I said that's enough. Luz, find your jacket, and I'll zip you up. And Joe, take your cane. You shouldn't put pressure on the ankle."

And so we set out, my four-and-a-half-year-old daughter as babysitter, or more aptly, guide dog as my cane tapped along. We held hands, and she chattered about something she'd made in preschool, a painting of a forest. Outside, it was dusk. It must have been a fine sunset; a pinkish-yellow glow still hovered in the air.

"It was nighttime in the painting, so I made the trees all black. The stars were silver, and the moon was light blue."

"That sounds beautiful. Did you bring it home so I can see?"

"No," she said. "Don't you remember we keep all our work in our cubbies?"

"Oh, of course. It slipped my mind."

She led me expertly to a newsstand where the man greeted me like an old friend. Amit, no doubt. He knew my name and asked how I was doing. Had Norah and the kids told everyone in the neighborhood about the accident?

"I watched your show last week," he said with a grin. "Very clever, the way you trapped that embezzler. And they threw the book at him."

At first I had no idea of what he was talking about, then I remembered I was allegedly an actor; I played a private detective if I could believe Norah. "Thanks," I said. "I'm glad you liked it."

On the way back I held Luz's hand tight as we crossed the avenue. I loved the feel of the small warm hand in mine. The trust. I must have been a good father, I thought with a touch of pride. If this was really my family. They must be my family, you couldn't enlist a kid as young and earnest as Kevin in some nasty plot. Luz prattled on about school, skipping along beside me. I didn't light up in the street as I would have done had I been alone. But I did as soon as we entered the house. Instantly I felt better as the drug swept through me, more confident. This would all work out. Surely the memory loss was temporary. I'd have it all back soon. Meanwhile, wasn't I the lucky one. I'd landed in a nice family: beautiful sympathetic wife, healthy, bright kids. I might have landed anywhere. Suppose I hadn't had any ID with me. I could have ended up in a homeless shelter. Or begging for change in front of a supermarket. Those were memories of things I'd seen, I realized. Memories. Odd what remained.

Luz said, "Daddy, if you smoke, you can die. They told us in school."

"I won't die for a long time," I assured her, "so don't worry. And I won't be smoking too much."

"Why didn't you know where Amit was?"

"I banged my head when the bike hit me, so I've forgotten a few things. But I'll remember everything soon."

"Did you forget me?"

I bent down to hug her. "How could I ever forget you, Luz? My best daughter."

"But you only have one daughter," and she laughed merrily.

I would try hard to be a father, and in time it wouldn't be difficult; after all, I'd done it up to now. They were good kids. I wanted to know them, to love them, if this was truly my home and I would be staying here.

IN BED THAT FIRST NIGHT I ASKED NORAH about Luz. "How did we come to adopt her? I mean her in particular." I asked her questions all the following nights too—we got into a routine we called bedtime stories.

"It was arranged before she was born. Her mother was a young Mexican girl. I wanted a girl so badly, I told you, but the doctor said it would be dangerous to get pregnant again. So we adopted her. Some people told me dealing with adopted kids can be difficult, but so far she's great. I adore her. And so do you."

Fine, I could believe that. She was an adorable child.

We lay quiet for a while. Did Norah expect me to make love to her that first night? Did I want to? Would it be like making love to an entirely new woman? Any woman I made love to in my present state would be an entirely new woman. What had my past been like? Lots of women? Few? Was I careless, left broken hearts behind? Or was I often the broken-hearted one? If we married fifteen years ago I couldn't have had too much of an amorous history, could I, in my early twenties? Why on earth marry so young?

Maybe the feel of Norah's body, the smell, the way she moved, would suddenly bring everything back—a new use for sex, as a restorer of memory. It was worth a try. But no, not just then. I was too stunned. And I had the odd feeling that any move on my part might be intrusive, as if I were a stranger unaccountably sharing her bed. On the other hand did she suspect there was something wrong with me, I mean something additionally wrong with me, lying next to a beautiful woman, and a willing one, I could sense, yet not making a move? Sex is not something one forgets how to do. I remembered it in the abstract, not any fuck in particular. That didn't worry me, though. It might even help me discover who I was. But we might have habits, routines, games, who knows? I didn't make a move. I lay still and silent and soon fell asleep.

When I woke, the window shades had been raised, and bright sunlight streamed in. I had to blink. I remembered the room from last night, but that was all: it was a room I had seen once, and sleepily. It was large and faced the street, a narrow street lined with well-kept brownstones. Respectable well-heeled people with respectable pasts. Was I one of them? Still, you could never tell. Lots of people looked respectable but weren't, and how did I know this? From childhood, somehow. And what did respectable mean anyway? For all I knew I'd spent time in prison.

The room had two bowed windows whose paint had been stripped down to the original wood. There were two dressers with mirrors, a Turkish rug on the floor, a couple of armchairs. Where did the money for all this come from? I must check into our finances, but not quite yet. Not before I've gotten the lay of the land. There was a small desk with a laptop, mine or Norah's, I didn't know. I didn't even know what she would use a desk for. What did she do? She could be anything, a research scientist, a rock singer, something in finance, in TV production? Opposite the bed, an open door led to what must be a bathroom—yes, I'd used it last night. Norah gave me a small flashlight so I could find my way around.

On the way home in the cab yesterday, she'd explained that we lived on the first three floors of a brownstone. She didn't say whether we owned or rented. If we owned it, we must have money. I almost laughed: I, a grown man, didn't even know how much money we had, if any. Earned or inherited? A glimmer of resentment against inherited wealth shot through me, again a flash from the past. I didn't feel like a rich kid, that I'd had a rich kid's life. But how could I know?

If the building was ours, we had to take care of it; there'd be tenants on the other floors. A new facet of my identity: landlord! Mr. Fixit. I'd have to greet my tenants if I met them on the stairs. Did I know how to fix things? Was I "handy?" I remembered the word from somewhere, a dust mote of the past, like a mote in the eye. Did I even know how the heating system worked? Well, that could wait. It was April. By the time we'd need heat, I'd be better. Or Norah would have stowed me in some rest home. How long could I expect her to live with me as I was? I wasn't much of a companion. It would be like taking on the care and education of another child, a large child. Another adoption. I could wash and dress myself, I was toilet trained, I could speak, but not much else.

I glanced over at the pillow beside mine, still dented where Norah's head had rested. Good. She wasn't a woman who got up and immediately plumped the pillow. Ah, I was showing preferences—the start of a self! I'd keep a close watch for more such signs. Of such small stuff identity is made. I knew that. Life had not been wasted on me.

We'd slept side by side. We started out barely touching. Once I woke during the night and felt her at my back, holding me around the chest. I would have liked to hold her too, but she was still a stranger. It would be easier to fuck a stranger than to cuddle up with her in the middle of the night. Even with no memory I knew that too. Very soon we'd have to make love. She would want to, at least I hoped so. I hoped that was a happy part of our marriage. Perhaps at the first touch it would all come back to me, what we liked, what we did. That was part of the body's memory, not the mind's. My body would know what gave us pleasure. Or was she the sort of woman who would tell me? The pain of not knowing these things gripped like a fierce muscle cramp. And then panic. What would I do from now on? How would I live? The enormity of what was lost spread over me, and I curled back under the covers. Not only my loss but theirs too, Norah's, the kids'. What could it be like to live with a husband or father who had no idea who he was, what he might have done or left undone. In some way their loss was as bad as mine. But at the moment I could focus only on myself.

What else did Norah and I do together? Did she run too? It was hard enough to believe I was a runner, with my ankle still throbbing, though more mildly than yesterday. She was in good shape, lean and lithe. Did we go to movies, restaurants? Did we follow tennis or baseball?

At last I forced myself out of bed but didn't know what to do next. My habits were gone. Did I take a shower first, or have a cup of coffee, or put on my shorts and go out for a run? Of course I couldn't do that now, with my ankle wrapped up. The cane leaned against a window, waiting for me like a patient friend. And then? Go to work? Check my phone? Read the paper? If I was an actor, as Norah claimed (unless it was a cruel joke), did I go to rehearsals?

I found a robe and went downstairs. Aside from Norah, dressed and in the kitchen drinking coffee, the house felt empty. She looked up questioningly, curiously, as if maybe the night had restored my memory and all was as it had been. I gave a tiny shake of my head, and she understood. She was still caretaker. The boys were at school, she explained, and she'd already dropped Luz at preschool. She'd usually be on her way to work now, she explained, but she'd taken a few days off to help me out.

"I didn't want to leave you alone in an empty house and not knowing anything. I love you. I suppose you've forgotten that too."

I had quite forgotten. I was getting a hint of what she was like. Tough-minded, often with an edge of sarcasm, not easily panicked. Those first few moments of the hospital visit were the only time, post-accident, that I'd seen her break down. I couldn't know about before. Generous. Efficient. Affectionate but firm with the children.

"What is the work you didn't go to?"

"I'm a research librarian at NYU. My specialty is the history of theater. I've been doing it for about eight years. I took a short leave after Luz was born, but I went back to full time pretty quickly."

"I don't know anything about you. I think I might fall in love with you. And how convenient. We're already living together."

"That's the kind of thing you used to say. You could be quite charming."

"I'm glad to hear it. Meanwhile, I don't know how to … proceed. I mean, what do I usually do first thing in the morning?"

"Pee, like everyone. They don't do that in books or movies, but trust me."

"Thanks, there are still a few things I know."

She said I went out to run most mornings, came home carrying a newspaper, showered, then read the *Times* in the living room. "At least on weekends. I usually leave while you're running. Monday was unusual. You went out to run in the afternoon because you had a script to read in the morning. You'd auditioned for a play." She poured me a cup of coffee. "Black, no sugar."

"Thanks. I guess I didn't get the part."

"You did, as a matter of fact. They called and left a message while I was with you in the hospital. Vince told them you'd had an accident and were in the hospital. They were sorry, but they needed someone right away. It was a new play, I can't remember the details."

"It doesn't matter. So I read the paper every day? Does that mean I'm a serious person?"

"Well, you devoted enough time to it. You read the editorials and checked the baseball scores and followed tennis. And of course the theater and movie reviews. You could sit with that paper for an hour or more. Sometimes I thought you were dreaming. Or hiding."

"Sounds reasonable. I have no idea what's going on, though. Are we in the midst of a war?"

"Nothing you'd call a major war, at least not here. But we have troops all over the place, Afghanistan for quite a while, Syria, Somalia. It's hard to keep up, frankly. I worry about what will be going on when Vince reaches eighteen."

That was a worry I could postpone for a while. I drank the coffee and helped myself to a croissant from a bowl on the table. "Look, I want to take a shower and shave, then let's talk."

"Sure. There's a lot to tell you, but one thing in particular can't wait."

Before I went back downstairs, I walked around. First I peered into the boys' rooms. The spaces looked as I'd expect, posters of athletes taped to the walls, computers on desks, crumpled socks peeking out from under the beds. A pile of boxed games, Monopoly among them, a few jigsaw puzzles, a chess set. Vince's? Kevin seemed more the type. I studied the bookshelf, which they shared: *Call of the Wild, White Fang*—which was the Jack London fan?—piles of school papers, and on what must have been Kevin's pillow, a ragged Curious George—I remembered him. I'm not sure what I was looking for. I just wanted a better sense of who they were, but these days that could only be found on the computers, and I wasn't about to invade their privacy.

I found a room on the third floor that looked like a study, mine, I think—there were old scripts and tapes labeled *Crime City* with dates. But it also held an ironing board, some folding chairs piled in a corner, and a closet with taped cartons. An ordinary house. Where were my secrets? Did I have secrets? Surely. Everyone did.

When I came back down, Norah poured us both more coffee and sat beside me at the kitchen table. "You need to know about this, Joe, for when you go back to work." She unfolded a newspaper clipping. But before I had a chance to read it, the phone rang.

She leaped up to answer. "Yes. Was it for tomorrow? … I'm afraid he won't be able to make it. He had an accident near the park and sprained his ankle … No, not too bad. I'll ask him to call and reschedule when he can get around better. Sorry. Give my best to Howard."

"Who was that?" I asked.

"Our lawyer's office. To confirm an appointment you had for tomorrow. I told them you couldn't make it."

"What was it about?"

"I can't say. Something you needed to discuss, I guess."

She lowered her eyes, and even without a memory I could see she was lying.

"You can tell me. Anything serious? Money?"

"I told you, I don't know," she snapped. "No money problems that I'm aware of. Now please look at this. It's important. About work."

Work. What sort of work could I return to with no memory? If I was really an actor, I was finished. Could I memorize a script? If I were some kind of scientist or mechanic I might still remember how to do my work. Muscle memory, again. Scientific knowledge would most likely remain somewhere or other in the brain. Probably the same with musicians or computer wizards.

The clipping read, "Actor Joe Marzino, 37, star of *Crime City*, was knocked down by a bicycle on Columbus Avenue near 77th Street yesterday afternoon and was taken to the emergency room at Mount Sinai Hospital, where doctors found a sprained ankle but no major injuries. The cyclist, Jose Rivera, 26, a pizza delivery man, was thrown over the handlebars and taken to the same hospital in critical condition. The accident is one of a growing number involving pedestrians and cyclists, which the mayor has been vocal about. Police blame the increase on electric bicycles used for deliveries. Transportation Alternatives says …"

So I was wrong about Norah and the kids spreading the word about my accident. Good, I wouldn't have wanted a family that broadcast our private affairs. Even this much publicity was too much.

And I really was an actor. She hadn't been kidding. Yes, the Actors' Equity card in the wallet.

"Can't you remember anything about the accident?

"No. Tell me."

"It was Monday around four. You were coming home from jogging in the park. Not your usual time, as I told you. The police say the guy on the bike was going in the wrong direction in the bike lane."

"I've always thought those bike lanes were dangerous. Lots of the bikers go in the wrong direction."

"Well, that's a memory," she said with ironic good cheer. "Maybe you're recovering."

"I remember lots of irrelevant things. Just not who I am or my life. What happened to him, the biker?"

She paused. "You were brought to the hospital at the same time. He didn't make it."

"You mean he died?"

"Yes. It was awful. His family was in the emergency room in a cubicle right opposite yours. They took him off for surgery right away, before they even looked in on you. The family was crying. I felt so bad for them. He wasn't wearing a helmet. Or maybe they'd removed it. I tried to go over to talk to them, but I lost my nerve. They were talking Spanish very fast, and I couldn't follow."

"If I hadn't come by at just that moment …"

"It wasn't your fault. He was the one going the wrong way. You could have been killed. You were lucky. He flew over the handle bars and landed on his head. You lost your memory. He lost his life."

I lost my life, too, I wanted to correct her. But it was not the same thing; I was a living, breathing man with a minimal identity. At least the cyclist's family knew what they'd lost.

"I still feel guilty."

"Apparently there was quite a scene. Typical New York. Some kids passing by found you both and called the police. The guy's pizza boxes fell out of the basket and the cops found pizza strewn all over the street. The kids were eating it." She giggled. "I know it's not funny, sorry. They called me from the ambulance, and I went straight to the hospital. Oh, your phone. I forgot." She opened a drawer in a cabinet and returned holding a phone. "You'd better check the messages."

As if from a distance, I noted that I used the phone automatically. I knew exactly what to do. Maybe I'd always been good at that sort of thing. There were a bunch of messages, most of them promotions. But there were several texts from a Jonathan Welles.

"Read about your accident in the paper. Glad it was just an ankle and hope you can make it to rehearsal this coming Tuesday. There's that new script for next week. If the ankle is no good, we can write in that you had some kind of accident and give you a cane. But we need you."

I showed Norah the text. "You'll have to tell me what this is all about."

"I told you, you have a steady job now. That's why we were able to buy the house. Your agent sometimes gets you a part in off-Broadway plays, though. Luckily you're not in anything right now. Anyway, your show, *Crime City*"—she said it with a touch of irony that I was getting accustomed to—"is on weekly but you rehearse for weeks ahead; sometimes they have to search out locations. What Jonathan means is you should show up at the studio on Tuesday. If it was some other location, he'd let you know."

"Tuesday? What's today?"

"Friday. It's next week. They'll send a car for you.

You're the star."

"What kind of show is it? Do I have to sing and dance? Lord, I hope not."

She laughed. "*Crime City*. Does it sound like *Guys and Dolls*? It's cops and robbers. You're a private eye. You sometimes tangle with the cops. You know, like Humphrey Bogart?"

She seemed to find the situation amusing, but I was getting more tense by the minute. How could I take on a role when I was having trouble playing myself? An actor must start with something. Your self is your instrument. I must have heard that repeated dozens of times. Another memory. Acting classes?

"We can watch it tonight, it's on every Friday. The kids like to watch and laugh at your antics. You're a tough guy."

"Is that what I'm like? I mean in real life?"

"No, I already told you, you're even-tempered. Tolerant. Maybe that's why you play the tough guy so well. Your repressed tough guy. That's one of the things I liked about you at the beginning, because my father was hell on wheels. Gone now, and I can't say I miss him. Anyway, on the show you're tough. Ralph Skellings is your name. And you're very physical. You don't hesitate to throw your weight around."

I was tempted to laugh. But just then the phone rang, and Norah raced to answer.

"Who?" I heard her say. "Oh, Carla, of course. I'm sorry. Things are a little crazy here with Joe's accident. I told you about it the other day, didn't I? I was on the way to the hospital when you called and couldn't really concentrate … Yes, yes, of course I remember. Something about the poker game?"

She listened for a couple of minutes, then said, "I'd

better put him on. He's right here. Yes, fine, except for a sprained ankle and a little mixed up about the time sequence. Hold on."

She covered the phone with her hand and told me, "Carla Landers. She's George's wife, from your poker game."

I shook my head. Empty. Not even a pebble bouncing around.

"Look, just talk to her. She called before, I can't put her off again. Do your best."

"Hello, Carla," I said, taking the phone. "How are you?"

"I'm fine. More important is how are you? Are you up and about? I read about your accident in the paper and called to see if you were okay, and also to thank you for what you did for George last Thursday after the game at our house. Norah said to wait a few more days because you were in the hospital, and it wasn't too serious. So how are you anyway?"

"A sprained ankle. Coming along all right."

"Good. Look, I want to say how grateful we both are. You saved George from what might have been serious trouble."

"Well, glad to help." I waited a moment then decided, the hell with it. Otherwise this would sound like a bad script. "Listen, Carla, there's something I should tell you. I was hit by a bike, you know, and suffered some minor memory loss. It will go away, but meanwhile I don't remember anything from a week or so before the accident. So maybe you could remind me of what I did for George."

"You don't remember? That's weird. It was so important to him. To us. Well, I'm sure it will all come back in a couple of days." She took a deep breath.

"George has a problem, you must know. The horses. It's been going on a long time, and I've begged him to go to Gamblers Anonymous, but he wouldn't. Now that he's had a real scare, maybe he will. He fell in with some dangerous guys and owed—still owes, actually—a lot of money. They've been dunning him about it, one guy even came to the house and scared the shit out of me. They said if he didn't pay up last weekend ... well, it sounded pretty bad."

From the little I knew about bookies I could have told Carla that George was worth more alive than dead. But first I wanted to hear about my good deed.

"He told you about it after the game, and well, the long and short of it is, you wrote him a check for $7500. That isn't all he owes, but it was enough to get them off his back for a while at least. We scraped together another $2500 and now he has a couple of weeks to get the rest. It was incredibly generous of you."

"Well, he's an old friend, and ..."

"And you'll get it back, I promise. I took on extra hours at the office, and if we get some help from my sister, well, it'll be all right. As long as he stops."

"Don't worry about my getting it back. Just make sure he stays out of trouble."

"Yes, that's what I'm trying to do. But it's an addiction, you know? He needs help. I mean professional help. I think he'll do it this time. He was really freaked out. It meant so much to him that you helped."

"Glad to do it."

"And Joe, there's something else ..." She hesitated. Not more money, I hoped. I was already worrying whether we had enough in the checking account to cover what I gave George. Norah and I still hadn't gotten to the subject of money. All I knew was that there were some twenties in the book, *The Theory of the Leisure Class*, where we always kept them. I remembered that, like I remembered where I kept my shaving cream and my old bank statements.

"That moment in the hall when you were leaving? I was feeling so relieved … And grateful. I'm so embarrassed at what I … It didn't mean anything, believe me. I had a few drinks too many, watching TV while you were making so much noise in the dining room, four guys with a lot of beer in them, you know, can be pretty loud … I hope you didn't take it the wrong way."

"Oh no, don't worry about it. Truth is, I don't even remember it." That wasn't very flattering, I realized as soon as the words were out. But at least it was the truth.

"Good. I don't know what came over me …"

"Carla, just forget it. It never happened."

Whatever it was. It couldn't have been more than a drunken kiss. Was I so irresistible? I started imagining a scene, making up things that might have happened but surely never did. Suppose she threw her arms around me and said she'd always been turned on by me, and could we meet some time and get to know each other better? This was absurd, not to mention distracting with Norah right beside me, and I let the curtain fall on it immediately.

I hung up and asked Norah, "Did you know I gave George $7500 for his gambling debts? We must have had a game last week."

"Yes, you told me that same night. I feel for Carla. The guy is totally irresponsible. This isn't the first time he's had to borrow. Don't count on getting it back any time soon."

"But can we cover that kind of loan?"

"Yes. I have a little nest egg I haven't reminded you about."

"Oh, is that so? What do you do on the side?"

"Nothing disreputable, I assure you. I'll tell you about it one of these days. First things first."

WE ALL WATCHED *CRIME CITY* TOGETHER that night. The younger kids were allowed to stay up late on Fridays. Norah and I sat together on the couch, our hands touching, not quite holding, Luz on Norah's lap and the boys sprawled on the floor in front of the TV, the kids eating ice cream—Luz making a mess of a chocolate popsicle that dripped on her shirt—Norah with a glass of wine, and me smoking. No one objected or waved their arms around—Norah must have told them to go easy on me.

The show was obviously inspired by *Law & Order.* It was engraved in some corner of my brain, like TV commercials one would rather forget. What was different was the dominance of the private detective, Skellings, that is, me, whose dealings with the police were ambivalent, like Bogart in his films. Rather than a trench coat I had a leather jacket. I did well; it was cheering to see myself competent at something. Convincing and, as Norah had said, tough. But fair. I flirted with the women involved in the plot, but it never went farther than that. The focus was on solving the crime—I didn't seem to have much private life. In the episode we watched, I had to find a drug boss who was using local kids to sell around the corner from the high school. He was contemptible, and I, as Skellings, was merciless, but didn't do much physical harm. At first the cops didn't appreciate my interfering, but when I caught him red-handed, they changed their tune. (Already I'm resorting to the tough guy cliches on the show.)

At moments I found myself confusing the real me with Skellings. I had to remind myself that someone was writing his lines; he was fictional, his escapades had nothing to do with my life. But I couldn't help imagining that he was my real life, and my domestic existence was the TV show. That he was the real me and I was living a scripted life, as in *The Truman Show*.

Because despite the differences in our natures and temperaments, Skellings and I had a lot in common. Our face and body, for instance. Our voice. But the biggest thing we had in common was that we had no past. Or perhaps he did. There was a vague hint that he had once been involved with drugs, maybe even been a cop, but he was reformed now. Clean and mean.

After the show the kids insisted on playing a game they called Favorites, apparently something they often played before bed. Norah said okay but only a few rounds because it was late. First was colors. I remembered all the colors and said my favorite was red. Norah's was blue. Luz's favorite color was pink, and Kevin remarked that all little girls love pink. "I don't care," she said. "Pink is best." My favorite vegetable was tomato, though Kevin, again the critic, reminded me that it was a fruit because it had seeds. I chose corn instead, which wasn't true, but it was the only vegetable I could think of. One of the hospital meals had included a mound of corn niblets. Norah's favorite vegetable was radishes.

"Are they even a vegetable?" I asked.

"What else?"

"Radishes are boring," said Vince.

"Not at all. They're very tangy. And such a nice color."

"Person?" Kevin called out.

The younger kids named friends.

Vince quickly contributed, "Samantha," then looked at me.

"Oh, your mom, of course." I was relieved to see that was the right answer. The kids seemed relieved too. Yet Norah gave me an odd glance, as if she had her doubts.

"Mom?"

Without missing a beat, "Your dad, of course." The ideal family. If I'd seen this on TV, I'd probably snicker. "Okay, that's enough. Off you go." She went up with them to help Luz, and I sat alone, smoking and staring at the blank TV screen.

I WENT UPSTAIRS SOON AFTER. THERE WAS so much missing, I didn't know where to begin. Norah must have sensed that. As we sat cross-legged on the bed, she brought over an old-fashioned photo album. "We saved these before we started putting everything on our phones. I kind of like having them in an album. I wish we still did that."

She opened to a photo of a young couple: a tall good-looking young man in shorts and polo shirt, hair rather long, a sign of the times, looking pleased with himself as he leans against a tree in a park, it could be any park, cradling a tiny baby.

"That's Kevin," she said.

The boy tugging at his mother's hand must be Vince. He looks like her, though Norah noted that as time passed he came to look more like me. He's holding a paddle and small ball, the kind of paddle and ball that gets tossed back and forth mostly on the beach and makes that terribly irritating, rhythmic noise.

How come I remember that awful noise, that clack

clack? How does the brain choose what will remain?

The woman in the photo—who I must accept without further doubt, not only on the basis of evidence but need, is truly my wife, as these truly are my children—the woman is quite striking. Young enough to be called a girl. I do remember that girls are now women from the age of seventeen or so, or even younger, but in my inner ear they're still girls. Her auburn hair is short and cropped like a boy's, like Luz's. She's broad-shouldered, strong, and wears a sexy sleeveless white dress, very short, and she's tanned. Leggy. Gorgeous, my wife in that photo.

She turned some more pages. Baby pictures, mostly. Occasional strangers. "I'll tell you about them later. I want you to see the kids as they were growing up."

The photos were just of the two boys. I suppose by the time Luz was born cell phones had taken over the job of providing nostalgia. Looking at them didn't shake loose any memories or create nostalgia; how could it? I was starting to love them—I think I can call it love—as they were now. But their past incarnations didn't do anything for me. Norah must have sensed that because she closed the book.

"You're doing fine, as a father, I mean."

"It's barely two days. Not much has been asked of me. Before you rate my performance, why not wait for something serious?"

"I know, but I can see you're trying. They'll be okay with it." She paused and was about to continue when there came a soft knock at the bedroom door. It opened, and Kevin entered in his pajamas, holding a book.

"I couldn't sleep," he said.

"You usually fall asleep fast," said Norah. "Is something the matter? Do you feel okay?"

"I don't feel sick." He looked around the room, as if

waiting.

"So what is it? Did something happen in school?"

He seemed to be near tears. "The teacher gave us this story to read …"

"Yes? About what?"

"A boy and a cow."

That didn't sound too scary, no monsters or wild beasts. A mad cow? He walked over to the bed and handed the book to Norah, who leafed through it.

"So what's bothering you about it?"

"Read it. You'll see."

"Do you want to read it to us?"

"No! You read it. From here." He pointed to a place.

"Okay, sit down here between us." She began to read in her low voice: "The small boy watches his father help the calf get born. As soon as the calf is dried off, the boy lifts it in his arms. He likes the warm feel of it, so new and fresh. His father tells him if he lifts it every day he will grow strong and will soon be lifting a cow.

"He does that, lifts it every day. The calf keeps growing, and the boy keeps lifting it. He lifts it every morning, just after sunrise, before milking.

"Day after day, from one season to the next, he lifts the calf. The boy keeps growing, but the calf grows at a faster rate, maybe because it has a shorter life span, so it has to grow faster to reach its full growth. One day the boy notices that it is not so easy to lift the calf, now almost a cow. As the days proceed, lifting it begins to get difficult. More and more difficult every day. Would it be easier to lift after it is milked, or would it not make much difference? he wonders.

"Every day after milking, now almost a young man, he strains harder to get the cow off the ground. The cow has grown heavier at a faster rate than the boy has grown stronger. He worries that there might come a day when he can't lift the cow. But how could that happen, from one day to the next? Why, if he has lifted it on a Monday, could he not lift it on Tuesday? The cow cannot gain much weight in one day. Meanwhile his father is getting older and tired, and the boy has taken over many of the chores the father used to do with ease.

"Soon the boy is lifting the cow only a couple of inches off the ground, and for a shorter and shorter time, until he is almost dropping it after an instant. Then a day comes when he just cannot get it off the ground. 'It's a full-grown cow now,' his father says, watching. 'No man can lift a cow.'

"This is very disappointing. Worse than disappointing. He had believed his father when he said he would be lifting a cow. He had thought it would be forever, till the day he died, or rather till the cow died, or more likely was taken off to be slaughtered. Nevertheless, the boy, now fully a man, has indeed grown strong from lifting the cow daily. He has grown stronger each day, until a day comes when he no longer grows stronger. He reaches a plateau. Then, very gradually, he begins to grow weaker, as his late father did. He grows weaker every day, until it is out of the question to think of lifting a cow and it seems impossible that he ever did."

He shut the book.

"So what is it? Do you feel bad for the boy?"

"At the end, where it says, 'his late father,' that means he's dead, right? Doesn't 'late' mean dead?"

"Yes."

"So his father dies, and his cow is taken to be slaughtered, and he has no one left." Kevin's eyes filled with tears, and he leaned into Norah's shoulder.

Finally I stepped in. "You were afraid I might have

died, right?"

He nodded.

"I didn't die. I'm right here. I only sprained my ankle, I was lucky."

"And you lost your memory."

"Well, only some of it. And it will come back."

"But when?"

"I don't know. But it will. But meanwhile I'm alive." I reached over and pulled him towards me. "It's a sad story, but it's just a story. It's not about us."

After a while he fell asleep between us. "This happens sometimes," Norah whispered. "He's very sensitive. Last year, after that terrible killing at the school in Connecticut, all those children dead, he didn't want to go to school for a week. I had to walk him there and stay in the classroom until he felt safe."

"What killing?"

"Oh God, don't you remember Sandy Hook? A suburban town in Connecticut. A gunman killed children and teachers, it was the only thing in the news for days, parents waiting outside to see if their kids were alive, and ... A horror story, teachers shielding the kids ..." She had tears in her eyes. "It made everyone scared to send their kids to school. A madman."

I was ashamed that I couldn't remember. I carried Kevin back to his bed. He was a nine-year-old boy, maybe sixty or seventy pounds, and I could lift him easily. But there would come a time when I couldn't.

"You can see how much you mean to him. If he lost you, or anything happened ..."

"Well, I'm here for now. The foreseeable future. What other disasters am I missing?"

"A lot. It's been a bad few years. A tsunami in Japan caused havoc at a nuclear power plant, like at Chernobyl, which you probably don't remember. Kevin heard a snatch of that on the news and was worried about it. And a couple of years ago an earthquake in Haiti killed nearly a hundred thousand people. As if things there weren't bad enough already."

That the world was a perilous place was not really news to me. But all of this seemed a bit like overkill, so to speak. It would be easy to catch up on the disasters, and even the basic facts of my life that Norah was trying hard to fill in. But already I had a feeling that something crucial was missing and would remain missing. Not something that Norah could help with. Something secretive. Something no one knew but me. If I didn't get it back, it would be lost.

And here I've been worried about my private life while the world was suffering all sorts of disasters.

"There's more, but I'll save it for another night. Let's try to get some sleep."

"LOOK, I HATE TO THROW EVERYTHING AT you at once," Norah began the next night. "I can imagine how hard this must be, but your mother's been calling. She didn't see the small article in the paper, luckily, but I called her right after I first visited you in the hospital. I thought it was only right, in case things got worse."

"How much did you tell her?"

"I just told her about your ankle. Not about the … the other thing. I thought that might straighten out after a day or two."

The other thing. She still couldn't say amnesia. Or memory lapse. Or anything nearing the truth. I remembered that people didn't talk about AIDS at the beginning. It wasn't a memory exactly, just something I knew about, just as I'd known who the president was. AIDS at the beginning was something to be dreaded, ashamed of. Before it got so widespread there was no hiding it. Maybe we had friends who'd died of it. Friends. Who were they? How would I behave with them? Even if I was an actor, I wouldn't be good at hiding my blank memory, and I hadn't even been out and met neighbors, or our tenants. Amnesia is debilitating too, but hardly life threatening. There isn't any life left to threaten—it's gone. There will never be activists agitating for a cure. It's not contagious even by sexual contact, though I have yet to try that. And still it feels shameful. Though it doesn't lead to death, merely, to judge by my own case, an occasional death wish. Still it is a kind of death, the death of a self without a replacement. A self isn't something you can trade in for a new improved one, like a car. (Which reminds me, where is our car, assuming we have one?) Or, say your house is destroyed in a hurricane and you have to rebuild. Except you don't have the materials. You stand in front of the site where your house once stood, looking at it, trying to visualize a new house. But you stand with empty hands, no tools.

You wait for a miracle.

"She's been calling my cell every day, and now she's asking when she can come over. I've been putting her off, saying you're tired, but I can't keep that up." Norah reached over me to take a cigarette from my pack on the night table and lit up expertly with my lighter. "Or she'll suspect something worse. Or think we don't want to see her. She's sensitive, you know?"

"Oh, do you smoke too?"

"I stopped when I got pregnant with Kevin, long

ago. But now, what the hell? I'll keep you company."

"So my mother is sensitive? What is she like? Isn't that awful, to forget your own mother?"

"Worse than forgetting your wife and kids?"

"A hard choice."

"You might remember something when you see her. She's young for her age, mid-sixties, I'd say, and in good shape. Probably goes to a gym or has a personal trainer. After your father died, she lost thirty pounds, learned to drive, moved out of the city, and went to work in a Nordstrom near her new place. She started on the floor, selling, and worked her way up. Now she's a buyer. She changed totally. Like she took a course in acting well bred. Naturally, she's very well dressed. Intimidatingly. I don't know how she does it. When she sees me in my jeans, she shakes her head and offers to bring me clothes. 'A good-looking girl like you, Norah, you ought to make the best of it.' Anyway, she's been widowed about eight years, but she's taken her widowhood very well. Your parents weren't, uh, the best of friends, I'm sorry to say."

Somehow this didn't come as a surprise.

"She didn't approve of some of his associates. When they came over for their poker games, they were too loud, and one liked to slap her ass."

"So how did my father die?"

"Well, that's always been kind of mysterious. She doesn't like anyone to ask about it."

"I don't get it. What did he have? Cancer? Alzheimer's?"

"He was shot. His body was found in an empty lot in the Bronx."

"Shot? What do you mean? Who shot him?"

She stubbed out the cigarette and took another one. She undid the pony tail. The auburn hair fell free over her shoulders, and she ran her fingers through it. "Look, are you sure you want to keep talking about this?"

"Just tell me."

"There was a bit of an investigation, but it never turned up anything or anyone. Your mother didn't push it. She said she didn't know anything about his work, just that he supported the family and that was enough for her."

"What are you not telling me? Was he a criminal?"

"All your mother said was that he was shot to keep him quiet. Your father was away a lot, you told me. Away on business. A salesman."

"Selling what?"

"I was never quite clear about what he sold. Something to do with machinery. Restaurant supplies, I don't know. Maybe you knew."

"*Death of a Salesman*," I put in, and immediately regretted it. He was my father, after all. How about some respect?

"I never met any of the poker players, but I thought there must have been something to do with organized crime, but it was never mentioned. Your mother never said a word, but she changed her phone number and gave up the apartment and fled to Westchester."

"You mean like *The Sopranos*? You must be kidding."

"You remember *The Sopranos*?"

"Yes. I don't know how. I remember books too. It's just my life, ha ha."

I was horrified and intrigued. It could have been an episode from *Crime City*. How would Ralph Skellings have handled this case? He would have gotten to the bottom of it, even if it involved violence. Was this story what was missing?

"Anyway, Willy Loman wasn't shot," said Norah.

"Your father was found in the Bronx. It was all pretty complicated, the inquest, the morgue, getting his body, and so forth. You managed most of it."

"Did I?"

"Yes, you did a very good job, too bad you don't remember. Maybe you met some of his associates. Luckily, they didn't attend the funeral—I think he was just a small cog in the machine. You wanted more of an investigation, but your mother begged you to leave it alone. He was gone, she said, and she didn't want you involved. So you didn't press it, and she was grateful. Even your sister was grateful."

"My sister?"

"Your twin sister, Susan."

"A twin? You haven't mentioned her before. Just when were you planning to tell me?" My face was growing hot. To think the past held so much, facts, data, not to mention thoughts, feelings, inclinations. I'd never recover it all. I'd always be the stranger in town. "A twin, for real?"

"Yes. You're right, I should have told you before. But look, you're barely home three days, and you're not in touch with her very often. I can't cover a lifetime. She lives on a ranch in Colorado and breeds horses. Oh, and she's gay. Your mother is not thrilled about that. Her partner's name is Monica. She's a potter, quite talented, Black, from Jamaica. You never warmed to her, or she to you. You found her too bossy with Susan, and she found us too bourgeois, typical white privilege, you know. Hard to argue with that. But you admired her, and loved to listen to her talk. You pick up accents. We have several of her things. That bowl I served the rice in tonight. This green and blue ashtray we're using. It's funny, I used to think I had a twin. But you're the one. I thought I might have had one who died at birth. Or a stillborn. Maybe she'd remained an embryo and was still tucked somewhere in my mother's body. I know that sounds crazy. But I wanted someone to talk to who would understand me totally and share my feelings exactly. I'd once heard my aunts talking about how my mother had had a miscarriage with twins. So maybe she'd carried twins again."

"Was I ever that to you? I mean understanding you totally, sharing your feelings exactly?"

"Well no, I can't say you were. But one can't expect that of a husband."

What about a wife, I thought. "But did I share your feelings enough?"

"Enough for what?"

"To make you happy."

"We're different," she said. "My expectations of life are lower than yours."

"You sound like you were lonely. Maybe you still are. Were you an only child?"

"No. There were four of us to start with." She paused and bent her head. "I can't—let's leave that for another night, okay? The more pressing thing is your mother. Plus you've got to prepare to see Jonathan."

"Wait a sec. I get the impression Susan and I are not on close terms."

"You are correct."

"Can you tell me why?"

"That's something else I'm not too clear about. She'd better tell you herself."

"Okay," I said. "Back to Mom then. Is that what I call her, Mom?"

"Yes. Mom—her name is Dorothy—is quite competent and in good health. But she's … sort of volatile, I mean emotionally. She has a short fuse, and you have to treat her with kid gloves. She changed after your father died. Anxious about everything. But you never knew anything about his business, thank goodness. So when she comes to visit, try to be careful."

"I can't hide the memory loss."

"I've already told her that. Not the whole thing but enough. I said it was temporary, which let's hope is true. She had a minor fit over the phone. She wanted to know who was the guy who ran into you, and when I said it was a young Dominican pizza delivery man, she was relieved, I'm not sure why. Maybe something to do with your father and his cronies. Then she asked if it was a 'nervous breakdown.' That's what she called it. I tried to explain. And then she was worried about your career. You know, Skellings. She's very taken with him. He's so attractive in that leather jacket, she always says."

We both smiled for the first time since this peculiar talk began.

"She was afraid he might be removed from the show, and you'd be out of work, but I said that was unlikely. You can still walk and talk." That same irony in her tone, as if she were alluding to the many things I couldn't do. Like fuck, maybe.

"Yes, if I'm no one, I can act like anyone," I said.

"That's the kind of remark you shouldn't make to her. And Joe, maybe you could try ..."

"Try what?"

"Try to act like you haven't forgotten ... everything. I'll fill you in. I mean, act like you know her and some things about her life."

"How is she with the kids?"

"Great. Especially as Susan isn't likely to have any. She loves them, always brings them presents. A doting grandmother. She's already thinking about the pretty dresses she'll bring Luz when she's older. You know, from her job. That would be in about a dozen years."

"So when is she coming?"

"We can have her over one day next week. I'll find out what day she's off. She lives in Westchester. It's a well-to-do suburb just north of—"

"Norah, I know where Westchester is. I wasn't born yesterday."

"Oh no?" she said. And we laughed again. I reached for her hand and squeezed it.

"Your mother has a car, but lately she doesn't like to drive in the city or drive at night. So we can put her in a cab to Grand Central."

"We have a car, don't we? Luz said something about driving to the Bronx Zoo one day."

"Yes, a Toyota RAV4. Tomorrow I can tell you where it's parked. I assume you can still drive?"

"We'll soon see. It's the left ankle. That was lucky, I guess."

LUCKY TOO THAT I WAS A RUNNER IN NEW York and not in Boston, because the next day the news was blaring about the attack at the Boston Marathon. Explosives. Right near the finish line, when the mid-level runners like me were coming in. Several people dead and many more injured. Norah reminded me that I had done two marathons in the past. The world that I had forgotten was indeed a frightening place. I knew the atmosphere of marathons well enough to be able to imagine the chaos, the screams, the bodies sprawled in the street. But it can't happen here, I thought with the stupid optimism of one who has forgotten the dangers of ordinary life. Someone to whom they were stories only.

Kevin was on his way up to bed, but he paused when he saw us, with Vince, staring dumbfounded at the TV screen.

"What happened?"

"This is unbelievable," Vince told him. "There was an explosion at the marathon. People were killed. Lots of them lost their legs."

Norah switched off the TV. I had a ghoulish vision of bodies lying in the street with severed legs strewn about. Could they be sewn back on? Or stapled, as the nurse had mentioned is done these days? How to make sure they matched up the right legs with the right people?

"Daddy," said Kevin with a tremor in his voice, "you're not running in the marathon this year, are you?"

"No, no, how could I with this ankle? Anyway, I haven't even trained. Have I?" I glanced at Norah for confirmation, and she shook her head, no. "No, don't worry about it. Anyway, this was up in Boston, far away."

As the news about the hunt for the perpetrators emerged, Vince kept his younger brother filled in on all the gory details: they were two young Russian brothers who fancied themselves terrorists: one brother was found hidden under a tarp in a rowboat in someone's alley, there was a car chase with the police through the Boston suburbs ... "And the older brother, who was driving, ran over his brother."

"He ran the car over his brother?" Kevin echoed in disbelief.

"Right. They finally caught him, the younger one, and he said he just did what his older brother told him." Vince ruffled Kevin's hair. "You wouldn't listen to me if I told you to do something bad, would you?"

Kevin shook his head as if the question were in earnest.

"They were so dumb, they didn't even have proper explosives. One of them was made from a pressure cooker, maybe they got it from their mom's kitchen."

"Do we have to be so detailed?" Norah put in.

"It's interesting, I thought. Isn't it, Kev?"

"It's horrible. So what will happen to the people who lost their legs?"

"They'll be helped in the hospital," I said. "They'll get prosthetic legs that attach to the body so they can walk. I think it's bedtime. Why don't I read you a nice story, something happy, like…"

"I don't think you should run in any more marathons," he said as I led him upstairs.

MONDAY MORNING NORAH REMINDED ME that the most important thing right now was to get back to work. At her urging, I texted Jonathan and arranged to drop in at the studio later in the week. Seeing him would be like meeting a stranger, while he would know me quite well, both as Joe the actor and as Skellings. This gave him a considerable advantage since I didn't know either one. If anything, I knew Skellings better: I'd been watching his old escapades. Over the weekend I'd sat with the boys around me, who seemed engrossed. I had my arm around Kevin—it felt natural, and I wondered if we had often watched this way. He seemed quite comfortable snuggling into my shoulder. He was a shy boy and didn't say anything about my being back, but as I got to know him I could tell he was relieved. A bit puzzled by the changes in me, no doubt, but most of all relieved. He was old enough to understand that it might have been worse. It would not be like the story about the boy and his cow, at least not yet. If I got up for a moment to get a beer from the fridge, he'd hand me my cane with a shy smile, even though I could manage without it around the house. Usually at around ten he was sent up to bed by Norah, who sat in the next room reading or fiddling with her phone. He'd kiss me good night, evidently he isn't too old for that, and I hugged him and grew teary at my luck. In shaky moments I had a leftover wisp of suspicion that this might not be my real family, despite the wealth of evidence to the contrary. And maybe what Norah had told me about my parents was a story meant to keep me from a worse story. Let's say I was trapped in a scheme that one day would explode in my face. Just let it not involve the Mafia—all I knew about that was from seeing the *Godfather* movies, and I didn't want any part of it. But the more time passed, the more I watched myself as Skellings, the more natural it became to accept this as my place, my life.

In a sense I was like a fictional character too, someone you might come upon in a novel. I might make up a past for Skellings as I could not do for myself—I already had a past, only it was unattainable. I'd think about his childhood and young manhood. When playing characters in serious dramas, as I no doubt had done, actors often make up missing parts of the characters' pasts, to make the acting more convincing. Skellings was not a character of such depth as to require much of a past, but that didn't mean I couldn't supply one for him. A project for a sleepless night.

Vince was full of commentary when we watched Skellings re-runs. He'd let out a whoop of approval at some clever deduction or quick move. "Cool, Dad!" He seemed embarrassed when Skellings flirted with secretaries or bank clerks in his efforts to get information. When on occasion Skellings casually kissed a clerk or even a suspect, he'd groan, "Oh, Dad."

"I couldn't help it," I'd say, grinning. "It was in the script."

I was impressed by Skellings' physical prowess. He ran up flights of stairs, gun in hand, scooted over rooftops, and in one memorable chase episode leaped from one roof to another, hardly something I could do now, if I ever could have. They must have used a stunt man. He pointed his gun frequently, as though to the manner born. Though he never used it, so far as I could see. I suppose if he shot anyone he might not be able to work as a private eye anymore, not to mention that he might lose his fans' approval. The cops he sometimes worked with used their guns frequently and, as in real life, often unnecessarily.

He arranged to meet shady characters in obscure corners of the city in order to gain information—thieves, prostitutes, drug runners, lowly members of the Mafia—one of these got himself killed for giving away secrets to Skellings. Whatever regret he felt was over quickly. One of his favorite places was a shoddy diner on Avenue C in the East Village, where kids sat out on the stoops smoking pot. Or sometimes the deserted West Side piers late at night, where he'd glance around warily while waiting for his informant. I rarely saw him in an office, like Humphrey Bogart's office in his glory days as Sam Spade, with his loyal secretary, Effie. Skellings was never shown at home. Usually at the end of an episode we'd see him climbing the steps of a brownstone, not unlike the one I was living in now, and opening the door with a key, but that was almost as far as any viewer was permitted to see into his private life. Except for a girlfriend, Cheryl, whom he saw on and off. She called his cell phone a lot, and he didn't always pick up. He usually saw her once during each episode, in a bar or at a movie. They were never shown in bed. (Could I possibly have a secret girlfriend I met in a secret place? I doubted that, but if it was true she'd be wondering where I am, especially if she read the brief piece in the paper. I found myself wondering about her, making up brief dialogues with her. And yet I hoped she didn't exist. Losing my life was already daunting enough. No complications, please. If she existed, she would turn up.)

What Skellings had to offer the people who met him in his shady spots, his suspects and informers, was his silence. He wouldn't tell the police their whereabouts. One prostitute gave him valuable information about a pimp who exploited recent female immigrants and kept them living in deplorable conditions not fit for animals: Vince's jaw dropped when he saw the half-dressed women curled up on cots in a shabby basement where food was brought to the door as if it were a prison. Even I, watching for clues about how to portray him, was gratified to see the bad guy locked up and the women freed. Many were very young girls from far-off countries who didn't know where to go next. Skellings, in one of his nobler moods, helped them locate family members through an immigrant service organization and brought a few back to their families himself, for which expeditions he wore slacks and a sports jacket instead of his customary black jeans and leather jacket, which I thought looked rather good on me. At such moments I felt proud of Skellings, as if I myself had done those good deeds; in my first week or so at home he was more real than I; he looked more comfortable in his skin—or I looked more comfortable in his skin—than I felt in my own.

He had a distinct identity, which I distinctly lacked. And why didn't I dress that way? I hadn't found anything resembling a leather jacket among my things, only casual, respectably dull urban wear.

THE HOUSE WAS QUIET THE NEXT DAY. Norah had gone back to work, and I was stretched out on the living room couch giving a first read to the script Jonathan had emailed me. Skellings was making a threatening speech to the man pressuring his client about a gambling debt, when our phone rang on a table near me. I hadn't answered the phone since I came home—they all spared me that.

"I'll get it," Vince called out from the kitchen. "Sandra?" he said. "Sandra … Oh, of course I remember you. Sorry. You used to babysit for Kevin, right? I guess for me too. Ha ha. So how are you? … Oh, really? Luz? She's fine. How did you know about her? Oh, I guess your aunt wrote you … No, Mom's out, but she'll be back soon. Should I have her call you? Fine, let me write down the number."

"Who was that?" I asked.

"Sandra. Our babysitter from years ago. If I hadn't remembered, it would have been embarrassing. She was just a kid then, living with her aunt around the corner. So now she's in nursing school in California and is here visiting her aunt for a few days. You probably don't remember them. She wants to drop over. Mom'll deal with it."

I went back to the script. It was a good one; the client was a white guy in his sixties in deep financial trouble, and I was eager to find out why, as the viewer should be. Also, I was glad Skellings didn't have as many lines as usual. The first reading was fun, seeing what my evil twin, as I thought of him, was up to. The real work would come later, not only learning the lines but figuring out how to deliver them, and depending on how I managed, could take most of the weekend.

Norah breezed in with packages. "You had a call," I said. "Some babysitter who used to work for us. Vince can tell you."

She dropped her packages on a chair. "Vince?" she called. Her voice was shaky. Vince came in and picked up the packages.

"Oh, yeah. Sandra called. I didn't even remember her at first. She's here from California visiting her aunt and wanted to drop over."

"Do you have the number? Give it to me."

She dashed upstairs, and I didn't see her for a while. Kevin came in; he'd been at a friend's place down the block. A neighbor brought Luz home from a play date, and she climbed on me until Vince settled her in front of the TV. So this was family life, people coming and going, enacting their roles. TV sitcom. Two weeks ago I must have been used to it; now it felt like a strange country. I read some more of the script, then went upstairs and found Norah lying face down on the bed.

"Is something the matter?"

"Nothing, it's okay."

"You don't look okay."

"Just a bit of a headache. It'll go away if I sleep a while." I went back to the script.

AND TO MY RESEARCH. WHEN I TIRED OF studying Skellings on screen, I gathered my courage and looked up, not for the first time, amnesia. On previous occasions I'd been daunted, but I was determined to persist. I remembered Google, the repository of everything. What if Google got amnesia, say someone pressed the wrong button? I suppose we'd have to return to written records, the dark ages. I hadn't forgotten how to use the computer, but the scientific and medical websites were complex. There are apparently several kinds of amnesia, and mine, retrograde amnesia, was reversible and not the most severe. Worse is anterograde amnesia: you can't remember things that happen after the accident or whatever caused the amnesia. Those people seem far worse off: how awful it must be to forget what happened an hour or five minutes ago. In that condition I would have remembered my entire past life until the jogging accident, but I would be unable to remember anything from day to day since, namely my family, my home, my job. There'd be no question of my continuing as Skellings, whom I'd grown fond of and would miss. I found a few famous cases of this kind, people who couldn't keep anything in their heads for more than a few minutes. One of the most well-known, H.M., whose condition occurred after brain surgery intended to treat epilepsy, eventually dedicated his brain to science. What a generous nature, I thought, considering what science had done to him.

Since I was—am—an actor, I discovered plenty of movies about amnesiacs. If amnesia is rare in life, as the doctors say, in films and novels amnesiacs run rampant, in disguise; you'd never know if you saw one on the street. No way to tell whose heads are vacuous. (Like Mafiosi, I thought, with a shudder.) I began watching these films. I wanted stories of ordinary people and what they did when they found themselves in my predicament. Maybe I'd learn something about how they got their memories back.

The most famous is the old tear-jerker, *Random Harvest*, based on a book by James Hilton. Kevin drifted into the room, watched for a half a minute, then drifted out, but I had Luz on my lap for company. Handsome and ageless Ronald Colman, having just served in the trenches of WWI, escapes from the mental asylum where he's been confined because of amnesia and finds himself stranded in London in the midst of a riotous celebration. The war is over. He picks up, or is picked up by, a chorus girl, Greer Garson, who takes pity on him, and under her loving care he regains his powers of speech, though not his memory. They fall in love, marry, move into a cottage in a village and have a baby. He finds work as a journalist. A new life. No clues for my case, where I was plunked down into my old life.

Ronald might have remained happy in his born-yesterday state if not for an accident involving a horse and carriage, causing a blow that restores his past totally. This could never happen, the medical websites say, and I'm surprised that James Hilton didn't check it out first. Indeed a second blow on the head might cause even worse and irreparable damage. But not for Ronald Colman. Turns out he is the scion of a wealthy industrial family. But irony of ironies—now he's forgotten the past three years with Greer. A double whammy. He's an executive in the family firm, and Greer reappears as his secretary. He has no idea who she is, but that's okay; all she wants is to be near him. After a few more twists of the plot, he returns to the village where they once lived. She's there too! At the door of their former love nest, as he puts the key in the lock (sexual overtones), shazam, it all comes back. They fall into each other's arms (the baby they had is conveniently dead). The whole thing is supremely clever on the part of the script writer and unfailingly touching. Sentimentality at its peak. And as far as probability, one hundred percent wrong. Alas, it doesn't have any clues for me. But I must have a soft heart. I'm happy for the reunited couple.

Vince passed through the living room near the end, stared at the screen for a few moments "What's that?"

"An old movie about a man with amnesia. He was in the war. The first world war. He falls in love with the same woman twice—he can't remember her from the time before." Vince shrugs and moves off. Kevin has already gone to his room, probably to play computer games. Only Luz sits on my lap, sleeping soundly, and Norah comes in and carries her off to bed.

The only movie that is not scorned for inaccuracy by the medical profession is *Memento*, which came out in 2001. Like H.M., its hero, a young former insurance investigator, has anterograde amnesia, and so while he can remember his past before the criminal attack that caused his amnesia, he cannot form new memories. Doctors and psychiatrists have praised the film for its accuracy, so unusual in dramas about amnesia. The hero's wife was killed in the attack that damaged his memory, and we meet him in a hotel room desperately trying to figure out who killed her. But since whatever clues he picks up each day would vanish from his memory, he develops an elaborate system of notes to himself, often written on his body. He wakes up each morning determined to pursue his investigation, but must start from scratch, reading his scrawled messages to himself. The movie was a critical success, praised for its original use of flashback, its division into color and black and white to indicate past and present, and its general suspense and overall cleverness. The plot, close to incomprehensible, at least to me, is full of twists and turns and false leads, keeping the viewer in the same confusion as the protagonist and cleverly reflecting the state of mind of one in his predicament. A crucial turn comes near the end, when we learn that our unfortunate hero has been acting according to gross misconceptions, deluding himself along with the viewers.

I was left feeling almost grateful for my situation, which clearly might have been worse. Unlike that poor guy, most people with my kind of amnesia recover their memories in time, if not altogether then at least partly. So I can hope. And ordinary knowledge, like how to use the computer or drive a car, or pitch a ball, remained. Just what the neurologist said after the MRI in the hospital: my case was common, a head injury. I had to see the doctor every couple of weeks to report on any progress. To report on who I was. Or was becoming. The website said it helps if the amnesiac is reminded of events in the past, but what Norah had told me during our bedtime stories didn't call forth any memories, only made me more puzzled and lost.

There's no shortage of novels either, and in that first week I had time to read. The best was a small gem of a book by a young Japanese writer, Yoko Ogawa, called *The Housekeeper and the Professor*, a repeat of the trope of the elderly ailing man who finds love of a sort with his caregiver. Nothing very original there, but the kicker is that since his head injury in an auto accident 17 years ago, this brilliant professor of mathematics can't remember anything for more than 80 minutes. He remembers his life before the accident, but for the past 17 years, 80 minutes has been his limit. So when the housekeeper comes to work every morning with her small son, she must reintroduce herself. Love does develop, a new love each day, but somehow despite his 80-minute limit the love grows and deepens, and the professor acquires a family, better yet a family who becomes entranced by the abstruse mathematical mysteries he reveals to them. And to the reader as well—the mathematical oddities and serendipities he explains are one of the delights of the book.

Here too, the story left me grateful. How awful if I had to be reintroduced to my wife and children every hour and a half. I wouldn't even remember the results of my research, all the books and films I've been devouring. If I'd done anything really bad I'd forget it, like the professor, but if I learned about it, I'd feel the shock and shame all over again with each reminder. Besides, it would make for practical difficulties—to learn again and again where I keep my clean socks, my keys, where is Amit's newsstand, what are my children like, and everything that makes a life. A new life every eighty minutes. On the other hand it might have its advantages. Anything regrettable I'd done in the previous eighty minutes would simply be cancelled out. Like my awkwardness when I ran into a woman from across the street on my way to the super-market, Norah's list in hand. She had to remind me that we'd served together on a PTA committee. Or like my weekly poker game. Norah has told me who the guys are—no noisy types, and she's never complained that any of them slaps her ass, though no doubt they look at it. She said they'd be tolerant of memory loss, as long as I still remembered how to play poker. Maybe I'll resume in a couple of weeks. If my experience with computers and cell phones is something to rely on, I imagine poker will have remained. How good I was at it was another matter.

Poker is not important. Who knows what else Norah might be keeping back? What was missing? If I ever got an inkling of who I truly was, I might be nostalgic for the memory loss.

AT NIGHT NORAH TELLS MORE BEDTIME stories. After the kids go to sleep, or at least to their rooms, maybe to play computer games, we sit on the bed, and she tells me pieces of my life since she's known me. Some sixteen years. A little at a time. To recount the complete story of my life over sixteen years, every incident and change, would take another sixteen years, never mind all the years before we met. Or things I forgot during the ordinary course of life and forgetting. Even if she told me only what I'd be remembering if the accident hadn't happened, that might take, say 8 years. Take off some time for minor things that happened when I was alone and never told her, small things, bumping into an old friend, or an argument at work, or a movie I watched on TV while she slept. You can't tell someone everything, even if you're close. She said I liked to go to ball games with a friend, and sometimes I took the boys. Good old Dad. It could take days to reproduce a ball game in detail.

And even if we spent years with her recounting my life, what she knew of it, what about my thoughts, the life within? Everything that is unrecorded, the sudden shifts in attitude, the flashes of insight, the things you notice on the street, changing your mind about a dozen things, the changing allegiances to people, ideas, the flirting with a new idea … All that I once knew about my twin sister. Norah couldn't know any of that, any more than I could know that about her. At the moment I knew nothing about her except what I could see. Norah had a life too, parents, sisters and brothers, a past. Thoughts. Opinions. Feelings. Tastes. Who was she aside from my helpful wife? What was it about me that she loved?

"Enough about me," I said the next night, sitting on the bed together. "Tell me something about who you are. Anything."

"I grew up near Hell's Kitchen. Do you know where that is?"

"Yes."

"Okay, so we didn't have much money. My father drove a truck. He was away a lot. My mother worked at a home furnishings store, selling things we could never afford. I was a latchkey kid. And then there were my two older sisters—they both live on the West Coast, and we don't speak often. And then my older brother." She paused and lowered her head.

"What? Didn't you get along?"

"We got along fine. But he was killed on 8th Avenue by a drunk driver."

At this news I felt slightly dizzy. I was shocked and sorry for her, but the dizziness alarmed me. Light-headed. I stretched out on the bed.

Norah didn't seem to notice. "It was hit and run," she went on. "They never caught him. Or her. The car skidded onto the sidewalk, and then they must have gotten control again and sped away. It was late afternoon, not too many people on the street. He was thirteen, my brother. I was nine. Things changed after that. We had been an ordinary family, more or less, but everything changed. My father started drinking, and my mother stopped doing stuff like shopping and cooking. My sisters went to the state university up north, to get away, I imagine. I had to take over."

My head still spun. Why was I so bothered? It was years ago. "A hit and run. That is the most despicable ..." I murmured. "Was he or she ever caught?"

"No, they rarely are. Anyway, I had a hard time because I also had my dance classes."

"Oh, you were a dancer?"

"I was quite good as a kid, as a matter of fact. I was

at SAB, the School of American Ballet. Balanchine's company. I saw him when I was a little girl, right before he died. I was one of the favorites. I was chosen to be in the *Nutcracker* every year—a big production at Lincoln Center."

"I wish I'd seen you."

She smiled. "Little boys don't go to see the *Nutcracker*. Anyhow, you probably wouldn't have been able to pick me out, with all the kids dressed alike."

"Your hair. I would have noticed that." I reached out and stroked her hair, which was hanging loose.

"Maybe. I loved my brother. He was a wonderful big brother. He taught me to ride a bike. He taught me how to read when I was four, just like Kevin is doing with Luz. He taught me how to hit a ball, not like a girl but swinging from the shoulder. He taught me how to swim at Coney Island—our parents would take us there on weekends; it was packed, blanket to blanket. I was never afraid of the waves. I'm still a good ocean swimmer. He was a boy who could do everything—sports, school, music, he played the clarinet, learned at school, like Kevin. We couldn't afford private lessons, but the school let him keep the clarinet at home. He would listen to artists like Benny Goodman and then try to imitate them. He had hair like mine, only closer to red." Her eyes were tearing up. "I hardly ever talk about him, I still miss him."

"Did you tell me about him before?" I asked.

"Yes, of course, right after we were married. You said you wished you'd had a chance to know him."

"I still do. So what about the dancing? Did you ever audition for the company?"

She gave a wry laugh. "What happened to me happens to a lot of talented girls. I started to 'develop,' as they say. I got breasts, hips, I got tall. You look more like an athlete than a dancer, the girls coach said. I cried when she said that. I could still take class till I was 15 or so, but there was no point after that—it was clear I could never aim for the company. So I stopped. I stayed home more and took care of the house, cooked and so on. My mother wasn't good for much. My father drank, but only when he was home, not when he was out on the truck. At least he could control that. They were furious about Tony's accident, that someone had gotten away with it. They never got over it, the anger as well as the grief. They're both gone now, never got a chance to see their grandchildren." She paused. "They were good people. They didn't deserve what they got."

"Who does? And you?"

"I carried on. I went to City College and then got into Yale, the drama school, where we met. I thought I could do musical comedy, even with the breasts and hips—you know, Balanchine's dancers have to look like sylphs, those girls starve themselves, but not all companies demand that kind of body. I took singing lessons. But just after graduation I got pregnant."

"Vince?"

"Yes. And you know the rest. I mean you used to know. It was the three of us after that. It was a bad pregnancy, and the first few months with a newborn are hard. I guess I lost my ambition. Or at least put it aside."

"I'm sorry," I said.

"It wasn't your fault. It was both of us. And somebody had to work, so of course it was you. You were good, you got small parts here and there. And you worked in a copy shop to supplement."

She lay back looking exhausted. We lay side by side for a while, not speaking, and then I reached for her. She turned to me, and we made love slowly, not much urgency at first, and then she gripped me and pulled me into her, and we both came quickly, and the moment she stopped moaning she started weeping.

"What is it? I thought it was good for you. Or are those happy tears?"

"You remember that phone call from Howard's office? When I canceled your appointment?"

"Oh, I never called back. I don't even know what it was about."

"You were talking about getting a divorce. You said you'd talk to him to 'explore' the subject."

"Explore? This is crazy. What's it all about? Why would I want a divorce?" This woman I just made happy. I was happy too. My heart was racing, and I felt flushed. What wasn't enough for me? What was wrong with me? What else, I meant.

Norah gave a bitter laugh. "You're asking me why you want a divorce? That's a neat trick. It's what I asked you when you mentioned it."

"Well, what did I say?" The words made me feel ridiculous.

"Something about the way we first got together. Something never quite resolved. But please, not now. I need to sleep." She turned away and buried her face in the pillow.

Could that be the missing piece? No, it was too absurd. Divorce was the last thing I wanted at this point. Could she be making that up? But why? I doubted that I could manage on my own. No, I needed her. And what about our car?

"SO YOU TOLD JONATHAN ALL ABOUT THE accident?" I said to Norah as I was preparing to leave for the studio. "I mean, does he know …?"

"Of course I didn't tell him about your memory, no. Just about the ankle. And I said you were a bit woozy for a couple of days. He didn't seem concerned."

By now I'd seen plenty of Skellings and the other recurring characters, a couple of them police detectives. I'd written down the names of the producers and writers and others involved in the show. Norah had told me Jonathan was thirty-ish, a bit younger than I, and had made his name with this show and was already thinking of spin-offs. Arrogant, honest, not much patience but fair, wouldn't tolerate sloppy performances. There weren't many rehearsals—everyone had to learn quickly. But they could last for hours, with the setting up of scenes and other technical business. And sometimes we had to travel to far-flung parts of the city. Jonathan wouldn't do them in the studio. He wanted authenticity. There was nothing more I could do to prepare. They sent a car to pick me up, and I watched the streets go by. Everything looked familiar and unfamiliar at once. Was I remembering? Hard to tell. The receptionist at the studio greeted me warmly, and I regretted that I hadn't thought to ask Norah her name. A moment after I arrived, leaning on my cane, a lanky young guy with sandy hair falling over his forehead and thick glasses appeared and gave me a half hug. Jonathan. He wore pressed jeans with a sharp crease, and a plain blue shirt. Like Norah, like so many people, he appeared confident, certain of who he was—a talented young man on the make. And he would make it, too.

"Hey, man, it's good to have you back. I asked you to come in because frankly I wanted to have a look at you.

You look fine. I'm glad it was nothing worse than your ankle. We should start rehearsing tomorrow."

"Good to be back," I said warily.

He led me to his office. On the way I passed a large open area that held what must be parts of the set, a police station, the steps and door of a brownstone that must have been Skellings' home, and various fabricated bits of Manhattan's shoddier parts.

He retrieved a folder from the mess on his desk and handed it to me. "You won't have to bother printing this next one, I made you a copy. Luckily we're two episodes ahead, the last only needed a bit of editing, so we haven't missed any shows. You have a lot of fans out there who'd wonder if you didn't show up. We'll rehearse Tuesday and Thursday and start shooting on Monday."

Today was Tuesday. I shuddered inside. "I hope I can get ready by then."

"Of course you can. You're one of the fastest learners in the business. You did one show with only overnight to learn it. Norah told me you'd lost a bit of memory, but this is brand new so you shouldn't have any trouble. I bet you'll be up and running in a couple of weeks."

"Speaking of up and running," I said, and waved my cane at him. "I can't do any fancy legwork for a while."

"That's fine. Instead of having you injured on a case, which would spoil your famous invulnerability, we wrote in a skiing accident. You took a weekend off to go up to Vermont with Cheryl. As you know, she's always nagging you to spend more time together. A skiing accident can happen to anyone. No fancy footwork. We have a stunt man to do the falling for you. This new script is conventional, a man is having his wife followed because he thinks she's cheating on him, but in fact her frequent absences are because she's moving money around from one bank to another before she leaves him for good. There's no other man, she just can't stand the husband another minute. She takes a shine to you, though, and you have to avoid climbing into bed with her."

I laughed. "Poor Skellings. He's had that problem before."

"He's just too damn attractive," Jonathan said. Could he be coming on to me? Unlikely. Best to ignore it.

IT TOOK ME A LONG TIME TO FALL ASLEEP that night, and when I did, I had a dream, or I should call it a nightmare, though it wasn't as frightening as it should have been. I was in a small airplane, and it was going down. First, we were all in our seats, and after a while there were no seats, just an open space, and we sat on the floor. We knew somehow that we were going down, we could feel it, but it wasn't rushed or violent, just a slow descent. I thought someone would come in from the pilot's cabin to explain, but there was no sign of a pilot or a pilot's cabin. People are reacting in different ways. One woman is crying, and her young daughter is trying to console her. One man is sitting still looking catatonic. A few men in a circle on the floor are playing a game of cards, maybe poker or pinochle—big burly men needing a shave, maybe like my father's poker buddies. They made a lot of noise but here in the plane they're playing quietly. It's quiet except for the weeping woman. We know we're going down, but no one does anything about it. I seem to be in the plane and watching at the same time. The scenery outside the window gets larger, trees, houses, a highway. I think maybe we'll be lucky and just bounce on the ground and walk away, but I also know that the fuel tanks would explode on impact and we'll all go up in flames. We keep descending, but it's taking a very long time. But it can't go on forever; any minute now we'll hit the ground, and that will be it. It's slow, we keep descending, and everyone knows there's no hope, so we just wait. I woke up as we were descending, so slowly, and for a few seconds I still had the feeling of being enclosed in a small space and slowly falling until I blinked and in the dark understood I was in bed with Norah beside me.

AFTER THE DREAM, I LAY AWAKE FOR A long time wondering about secrets, what secrets my brain was keeping from me. Secrets worse than a secret affair. Shameful things I might have done. The way Skellings seems to have a secret. For every now and then there was a hint, from one of the cops he dealt with, that Skellings might once have been on the force but was dismissed for some nefarious act; how serious wasn't explained, but it must have been serious enough to have him thrown off the force. Murder, theft, drugs, planting evidence? I cycled through the possibilities as I watched him, but never found out, as viewers were also expected never to find out.

Are the secrets still my secrets if I can't remember them? But the acts exist. What happens to a secret that's never told, if the person dies never telling anyone? Does the secret still exist anywhere? In novels and films the deathbed becomes a place for revealing secrets, about parentage, money, treachery. Maybe it's just too hard to die keeping a secret, an act that simply disappears, although its repercussions may exist. And those who suffer the repercussions never know the secret that has rerouted their lives. I had an old friend who grew up never knowing that the aunt who raised him was really his mother. He said it changed his whole past, and his future too. (A memory! Discrete but encouraging. Not the right time to follow up.) How ironic that I remember someone else's secrets but not my own.

Have I lied, cheated on my taxes, stolen money (like the guy in the next script, it happened)? Have I been unforgivably cruel to anyone? Maybe I was the kind of boy who delighted in torturing weaker boys, in humiliating them, something I find contemptible. Was I arrogant, smart-ass? Or tough, like Skellings? A leader or a follower? A druggie? Probably not. I'd be having withdrawal symptoms now. Only the cigarettes, which in the face of this seem insignificant. I could have done anything, been anyone. Spent time in prison. Would Norah tell me? Or my mother?

SINCE I GOT HOME, I'VE BEEN PRETENDING I know the neighbors, chatting with the tenants in the hallways—luckily no complaints or repairs needed— with Norah filling me in or coming to my rescue when she hears voices in the hall. She hasn't mentioned the divorce, and I certainly won't bring it up. Meanwhile, my friend Saul comes to pay me a visit. Norah says she couldn't put him off any longer—he's been calling, full of concern. "You'll enjoy seeing him again," she said. "You were always very close with Saul. Way back even before grad school, a long friendship. He didn't go into the theater. He became an English professor and teaches mostly drama. He writes plays and teaches at Sarah

Lawrence. That's a college in the suburbs," she adds, since I must have had what she calls my blank look. I don't bother saying that I know what Sarah Lawrence is. The blank look is about Saul.

I open the door to a tall, hefty guy with a small dark beard, wearing chinos and an old sweatshirt and sneakers. I think I catch a whiff of cigarettes. He greets me heartily, shaking my hand, then a bear hug.

We settle in the living room, and Saul accepts a beer from Norah, who soon leaves us alone. He makes small talk for a while, and I do my best. I've been watching the news on TV so I don't seem like as much of a Martian as I otherwise might. After a couple of minutes of awkward silence, I say, "Listen, Norah might not have told you, but I had a head injury. I know we're old friends, but I can't remember much about you. It'll go away, but meanwhile, help me out here. Remind me of some stuff."

"Norah mentioned that. But I didn't think it was so …" His blue eyes widen, and his brows are furrowed. "That's tough. But sure."

Saul reminds me that in the Yale drama school we attended together he had focused on playwriting, but so far only one of his plays has been produced. A comedy based on his own mixed-up family. So he's glad to have the teaching job: comparative literature.

"I even tried a script for *Crime City,* and you put in a good word, but no luck. We used to play squash together. I usually won," he said. "You were too thoughtful. And at school we both dated the same girl for a while." He laughs. "Rosalie, her name was. She was very dramatic looking, long dark hair she swished around, big boobs, hippie clothes, leather boots even in summer. We both wanted her, but you got her," and he laughs awkwardly. "When you got tired of her, she came to me."

I smile, but nothing comes back.

"There was a little scandal while we were there. One of the professors came on to the guys. Not you or me, I guess we weren't his type. Anyway he had to resign in disgrace."

After a pause, he tells me that I got the part of the younger brother in *Long Day's Journey into Night* and confided in him that I didn't like the character. "But you did a good job anyway," he said. "You even did a bit of Shakespeare. Hotspur. You wanted that part really badly. Everyone thought it would go to George Drew, who was really better suited for it, but you pulled a fast one. You started a rumor that he was a dealer—I mean, he did sell some pot but only on a small scale, to his friends—but somehow it got back to one of the professors. He was too good a student to throw out—he's done very well actually, he's starring in an off-Broadway production of *The Master Builder*—but in any case the rumor cost him the part, and you got it."

"No. I really did that?"

"You really did."

"Shit."

I couldn't think of anything to say. Was I basically a nasty guy, someone who's become successful by lying and cheating and not giving a damn about others? Like Harrison Ford in an old movie, *Regarding Henry*, Norah and I watched it together in bed just a few nights ago. Brusque, snappy Harrison Ford is a lawyer who specializes in getting hospitals and other institutions off the hook when they really should pay damages to victims of incompetence. He has some kind of accident and awakens having forgotten everything, like I did. But there's an astonishing change in him—he even combs his hair in a new way, a middle part, suggesting innocence.

From being the hard-nosed attorney, the strict father, and the negligent husband, he's kind, generous, patient; he even delves into his old cases and tries to reimburse the people he's cheated out of what was due to them.

There was a character who changes entirely. Where does this new nice guy come from? Was he hidden inside or what? Why didn't amnesia make me a better person? Or maybe it did—maybe this was my better self.

While I'm digesting that truly nasty bit of information about what I did to get a part in a play, wondering what I must have been like—still might be like— Saul shifts uneasily in his chair and finishes his beer. "Listen, Joe, I recently read this book and thought of you, of what Norah told me. A novel called *I'm Not Stiller*, by a Swiss writer, Max Frisch? Did you ever hear of it?"

"No."

"I brought you a copy. You might find it interesting." He takes a book out of the backpack at his feet and hands it to me. I glance at the yellow cover, just words, no illustration, and put it down.

"Why?"

"You'll see when you read it. I don't want to spoil it for you. When I heard about your … situation, it reminded me of the book. I'm going to use it in class. I'm curious to know what you think."

We continue for a half hour or so, but it's not easy. I think of taking him out back to the small patio and garden for a smoke, but frankly I don't want to prolong the visit. I seem to have lost my social skills—such as they were—along with everything else. He's making an effort, but whatever I felt for him before, the hearty tone doesn't appeal to me, to whoever I have become, that amorphous me taking shape like a figure emerging from a fog, still barely visible. That figure doesn't seem like someone who'd betray a friend. Would my friends have done that? If I had any?

After a while Saul gets up to leave, hugs me again, and wishes me all the best.

"I'll see you again soon. Take care of that ankle, man, so we can play squash. Say good-bye to Norah for me." He's so eager to get away he almost trips on the four front steps.

THAT EVENING AFTER THE KIDS GO UPSTAIRS, the boys having watched a couple of last year's *Crime City* episodes with me, I start reading the book in bed. It takes place in Zurich where the police have picked up this fellow, Stiller, for something unspecified that he might have done. But the man insists he's not Stiller. Every indication says that he is Stiller, they have all the details about his past, they threaten to bring in his wife, to no avail. The guy is clearly Stiller, but he denies it. I don't see what it has to do with me, but it's intriguing so I persist.

Finally Norah comes to bed. I'm glad to see her—I want to get back to our bedtime stories and have her fill me in on our early days.

I barely give her a chance to get settled before I ask, "How did we start?"

"You mean us? How did we meet? People always like to know that about other people."

"This is not other people, though. This is us."

"You're right. Okay, you'd just started at the Yale Drama school, and I was in my senior year at the college. I had a job in the library, and you came in a lot. We … we got to talking and so it went."

"We got together?"

"Right. I got pregnant. We didn't know what to do. I was scared to have an abortion. Petrified. I knew a few girls who'd done it, but I had a bad experience with a friend. I stayed overnight with her right after she'd had an abortion. It was awful, she groaned and threw up and bled all over the place, and I called an ambulance. She almost bled to death, but she was okay in the end. Still, it scared the shit out of me. You were good about it. You said, all right, if that's how you feel, have the baby, and we'll take care of it. I don't think you really loved me, but you were willing to be decent about it. A good Catholic boy. You would do the right thing."

Somehow that didn't sound like me. "Decent? Did I say we should marry? Or live together?"

"I was never sure what you meant. You didn't say you loved me. But it seemed I could trust you to help me out with the baby, and that's what I needed at the time. And money. My family didn't have any money at that point. I didn't want to tell them unless I had to. Your parents were better off. As time passed, it was your idea to move in together. You said we get along well, and we might come to love each other. The sex was good."

"We must have been absurdly young. It doesn't sound like how I think of myself. But then how do I think of myself?

"Well, we did it. And pretty soon we sort of ... fell in love."

"Sounds like a soap opera. Or rather an arranged marriage. That's what they used to say about arranged marriages, that they'd come to love each other. Remember that scene from in *Fiddler on the Roof*? That song? 'Do you love me?'"

"Yes. So you remember that."

"I'm good with songs."

"Well, they put that on at Yale. You were in it. It wasn't a speaking part. You played a guy in a bar scene."

How many other parts had I played and forgotten? How many men had I pretended to be?

"Maybe it's true about arranged marriages," Norah went on. "Maybe it was better that way. My oldest sister has been married and divorced twice already, and at fifty that's no picnic. I often wish I could arrange a marriage for her. But back to us."

"Right." I was like a newborn, a large baby in a man's body. But Norah was sensible as always. Our life together was an essential lesson for the infant I was. There would be time for family trees, the sisters and the cousins and the aunts. And maybe a miracle would occur, and my memory would return, as the scientific research said. Then I wouldn't wake in a sweat in the middle of the night from a nightmare about being in the wrong family and waiting for one of them to hit me on the head with a hammer.

"So we fell in love?" Sweet, if hard to believe.

"Yes, after Vince was born. You were there in the room when he was born, and after that it was like a honeymoon, suddenly in love, with a screaming infant in the background. It was funny, looking back. Not at the time though."

"So how has our marriage been? Was it a good marriage? Would you call it a happy marriage?"

"I'm not sure what to call it. There were phases, I guess as in all marriages. There was certainly love, but there were problems. You can imagine, you're a beginning actor, and there's this baby…"

"So have we been faithful?"

She hesitated. "For the most part."

"For the most part, what does that mean? You're either faithful or not."

"How about saving that for another night?" She turned around and curled up under the blankets. I don't know how much time had passed—it couldn't have been very long—but when we woke we were wrapped in each other's arms. It simply happened. I forgot that I'd forgotten everything. I was the man I always had been, at least I felt I knew myself in this way. Everything was easy, slow, exciting. I knew just what to do, and so did she. Very slow, though, as if we were exploring. Before I knew it she was sitting on top of me, bending over to kiss me, the gorgeous hair falling on my face, and I heard her familiar sounds. I didn't know if I was remembering or not, but I certainly wasn't hearing them for the first time. She was no stranger. Our mouths were together the whole time, a long time. She stayed on top of me for a long time too, after, smoothing my hair and face as if I were a hurt child. She was crying. "It's so good to have you back. I didn't know if we would ever do this again."

"But of course we would. I wouldn't have been able to resist you for long."

"Ah, gallant Joe." And she laughed. "Really? And you still want a divorce?"

I didn't know what to say. "I can't remember that I ever did."

"Are you remembering anything?"

"I'm remembering the last fifteen minutes."

"You know what I mean …"

"I don't know. I forgot that I couldn't remember."

"Now everything will be different. You'll see. You'll get better."

I FINISHED READING THE SCRIPT WE'D BE starting to work on; I was surprised to see I already had some of the lines in my head. Then I replayed an old episode. I needed to take a closer look at Skellings, how he walked, his mannerisms, the way he held his body, the way he sat. The way he spoke: that turned out to be easy. His voice was mine, I hadn't attempted any disguises, though he spoke in a snappier manner than I did. He was all brusqueness, impatience, no time waster. What was his hurry? I wondered. He had a habit of stroking his jaw while he thought or listened, not terribly original, but I couldn't change it now. He occasionally picked at his fingernails. Rubbed his eyes as if he needed more sleep. This would all be easy to incorporate.

Kevin was sitting on the floor nearby as I watched. "Why are you watching this old one?" he asked, and I explained.

"Can you remember all that?" he asked.

"Sure, that's an important part of the job. It's not only reciting lines but creating a person who seems real."

"Do you get those things from watching other people, or just make them up?"

"Both," I said. "Right now I'm not doing anything but Skellings, but if I had a new part, I'd probably start studying people and looking for things to imitate."

"Cool," he murmured.

The episode I'd chosen at random from the stash in the study happened to be about a kidnapping. A boy from a rich East Side family, about nine years old, disappeared during recess, which was held in Central Park, not far from the school. He'd been playing base-ball, way out in left field. The teacher didn't notice he was gone until one of the kids alerted her, when he tried to throw the ball his way and realized the position was empty. No one had seen any strangers lurking about. Behind left field was a dense clump of bushes, and of course they all looked there first; then the teacher called the school, and they called the police. The parents were off in Aruba, probably making more money at the casinos, but the nanny was home with a younger child. The parents returned immediately, stunned and furious at the school. A ransom note arrived asking for a huge sum of money. The police were stumped, and Skellings, summoned by the father, stepped in. A while ago Skellings had conducted an investigation of missing funds at the father's corporation—they hadn't wanted to get the police involved—and had the mystery solved in a couple of days, earning the father's admiration. The guy even offered him a job in the auditing department, but Skellings refused despite the high salary—not exciting enough for him. "I'm not an organization man," he'd replied, loosening his tie, worn for the visit to corporate headquarters.

Needless to say, Skellings found the kidnappers, with the help of some of his shady contacts. He snatched the evildoer just as he was picking up the ransom money left near a certain tree in the park, in an envelope covered with leaves and branches.

He found the boy quivering with fright, in a dank apartment on the Lower East Side, and bought him ice cream and a video game on the way to delivering him back home to his grateful parents. Skellings had a soft spots for kids, it appeared. The mother, a hysterical blonde with big hair, snatched the boy up in her arms. The father, gray-haired, round-bellied, and stoical, studied him as if looking for visible damage.

Kevin seemed frightened by the episode. He too played baseball in Central Park with the Little League, and I suppose it had never occurred to him that kidnappers might be lurking.

"No need to worry, kid," I reassured him, and tousled his hair. "No one will kidnap you. We don't have enough money to make you worth it."

As I said, it I hoped it was true. Strange that I hadn't yet mentioned that to Norah. I didn't know if actors earned a lot, or what she did at her librarian's job; that couldn't be much. Did anyone leave us money, a rich uncle? We'd need a night of storytelling on the subject of money.

I SPRUCED UP FOR MY MOTHER'S VISIT— fresh shirt, clean jeans, a shave. She fell into my arms as I opened the front door, which surprised me. Norah had said she was not especially demonstrative except with the kids.

"Let me look at you," she said. She used a tissue to brush away a mascara-laced tear. "When I think what might have happened … You look fine. How do you feel?"

"Fine," I said. "You look great." I tried to hide my disappointment. I'd had expectations. She was my mother, after all. I must have secretly hoped that the sight of her would bring everything back. But no. This aging but still firm body (a personal trainer?) was where I had gestated and grown into a person. But she was a stranger. She looked just as Norah had described her, and wore an elegant black and white print dress, summer silk, Norah told me later. And a big black straw hat she tossed on a chair. She was my mother, I should know her inside and out.

Once she was assured that I was alive and well, after a quick kiss for Norah, she fluttered over Luz. The boys weren't yet home from school. My mother sat in the living room with Luz on her lap. Luz liked to sit on laps, I'd discovered. She climbed on people, even her older brothers.

Thanks to Norah, the visit went along reasonably well. With relief, I found I liked my mother, and oddly enough, she reminded me of Norah, a sharpness of speech about her. But there was a touch of pretentiousness about the way she spoke and handled her coffee cup that was not at all like Norah, whose manners and movements were blunt and unadorned. She refused the rich pastries Norah passed around: "Oh, I couldn't possibly. I wouldn't fit into any of my clothes." Maybe she had a boyfriend to stay shapely for; I'd ask when the right time came. Not today. I ate one gooey pastry after the other, just to have something to do. I didn't want to smoke and have to listen to her chiding. I could manage a couple of hours this way and pick up some information. But then something happened that threatened to turn our family sitcom into farce.

There was a knock on the door. Norah went to answer. I heard greetings, exclamations of shock, women's voices raised. She ushered in two people who could only be Sandra and her aunt Rosa. Rosa was a small rotund woman in a light blue pantsuit with a large gold cross on the mound of her chest; she had a pretty, plump face beginning to wrinkle, and her dark hair was in a severe bun. Sandra was slightly overweight, wearing jeans so tight they looked painted on her, and a sleeveless Lycra shirt hugging her large breasts. She had long messy dark hair, curly and tangled, and wore enormous silver hoop earrings. She could have been a hooker. Luz's mother? It seemed incredible. I remembered my manners and rose from the chair. Rosa looked uncomfortable, and Sandra looked angry, while Norah made civilized introductions all around. My mother did not rise but responded politely though she seemed puzzled. She didn't know what was in store. No one did. Luz looked around casually but was more interested in the donut she was eating, licking the chocolate off her fingers and wiping them on her shorts. This didn't stop Rosa from walking to her and giving her a big hug. "Hola," she said, and something else in Spanish that I didn't understand.

Norah said how pleased she was to see them. She asked them to sit down and offered coffee. They refused.

"We can only stay for a moment," Rosa said. She had a low, pleasing voice and spoke with a heavy accent. "Sandra is visiting from California, and she wanted to say hello."

Rather than saying hello, Sandra flew into action. She dashed over to Luz, on my mother's lap, and snatched her up, donut and all. She began speaking to her in Spanish, low cooing phrases. Murmurs. Luz was startled and looked like she might burst into tears.

"I'm taking her home," Sandra announced. "I need to be with her." And she headed for the door.

"Wait. Let me," Rosa said. "I'll take care of it. She's been acting a little crazy. I'll go home and reason with her."

"I'm going with you," said Norah, at the door. "She can't do this. If only she'd asked." In a moment they were gone. I stood like an idiot. Should I follow? I didn't know where Rosa lived, though Norah had said it was very nearby. But I couldn't leave my mother alone, baffled. Her mouth had dropped open, and her eyes, gray like mine, were wide. To my surprise, she fumbled in her purse and took out a cigarette. So I'd been raised by a smoker. My fears were unfounded.

"Well, are you going to explain? Some stranger just ran away with your child."

"They're neighbors. Actually Rosa is Luz's great-aunt. Sandra used to be our babysitter."

"That doesn't explain anything. That girl seemed out of her mind. I'd go after her if I were you."

"Norah will manage. She knows them better than I do." I didn't want to say I didn't know where they lived. I'd never felt so stupid or helpless in my whole life. Though I was in no position to say that. I only hoped it was true, because this was pretty bad. "Let's just wait a few minutes. Meanwhile, tell me how you are. Norah says you have a very good job as a buyer."

"If they're not back in a few minutes, you should go get them. The job is the same old thing. I've done it so long now. Every season the fashions change, and I've got to keep up, but that's not hard. I like that part. Yesterday, I went to see my mother-in-law. Your grandmother. You do remember her, I hope?"

"Of course," I stammered. "But I've forgotten how old she is."

"Ninety-three. And looks like she'll go on for a while. She's lost a good bit of her memory, but she still knows me when I visit, and she asks about you and Susan. You adored her when you were a small boy. She told you stories and sang songs—she was quite a character. She's in a nursing home not far from where I live. If I tell her stories about the past, she starts to remember."

If only that were the case with me. Tell me stories, Mom. I wished I could remember this woman I once found so entertaining, but as with so much else, the stories and songs were gone.

"When you're more settled you might drive up and visit. She always likes to see you. Now you're the one who entertains her."

"I entertain her? How?"

I could hardly concentrate, I was so horrified at what had happened. It could have been straight out of *Crime City*. Where were they? Where was Luz? But I must keep pretending. Acting the role of son.

"Oh, you tell her stories about acting. Do you know she watches your program religiously? I think she mixes you up with your detective, but it really doesn't matter at this point."

"No, I guess not. I sometimes do that myself," I said.

"That sounds like the old you."

Maybe I'd take her suggestion and drive up to see Grandma. Wouldn't that be a scene, two people, once close, who've lost their pasts, trying to communicate?

Norah returned, looking haggard. A strap on one sandal was loose, and her shirt was rumpled. Had there been a struggle? It was more and more like a scene from *Crime City*—I imagined two angry women tearing at each other's hair and clothes.

"What happened? Where's Luz?"

She fell into a chair. "She says she just wants to hold her on her lap for a little while. Rosa calmed Luz down, and she was okay when I left. I said I'd be back in ten minutes."

"I'll go with you."

"Yes, you'd better," put in my mother. "This is actually kidnapping. You might have to call the police."

Better to call Skellings, I thought. He always knows what to do.

"I don't think it'll go that far," Norah said.

But it did, almost. Just then the door slammed, and

the boys came in.

"We've got to dash out for a minute," I said to them. "Keep Grandma company. I'll explain later."

Rosa lived right around the corner, it turned out, and I dashed as best I could with my bad ankle.

We climbed the stairs of the brownstone and found the door unlocked. Norah strode in, and I followed her into the cluttered living room. There were religious pictures on the walls and a large ornate cross over the fake fireplace. Sandra was holding Luz on her lap and murmuring to her. When Luz saw us, she tried to get up. She was whimpering. But Sandra held on.

"We're taking her home now," Norah said. "If you want to see her again, call, and we'll make an appointment. But that's enough for today."

"She's mine!" Sandra cried.

"Luz, come over here to Mommy."

Sandra clutched her tighter, and Luz cried harder. "You're hurting me."

Rosa tried to intervene and reached for Luz, but Sandra turned her back and shouted, "No!"

"You try," said Norah.

I went over to Sandra on the couch. "You know this isn't right, Sandra. You can't change things now. Luz," I said to her. "Come here to Daddy."

She reached her arms out to me and struggled to get out of Sandra's clutches but couldn't. I almost slapped Sandra's face but held back. I finally put my weight into it and yanked my wailing daughter from her embrace.

"Don't ever do anything like this again," I threatened. "If you do, we'll call the police."

Sandra burst into tears. "I didn't know what I was doing back then. When I let you take her. I was a child. It was all a mistake. I want her back."

Luz clung to me, her arms so tight around my neck I was almost choking. "It's too late. I'm sorry. If you calm down, you can visit her another time."

"No," shrieked Luz. "No visit."

"Not now," I told her. "Maybe when you're a big girl."

"No! She scared me."

Sandra wept on the couch while Rosa escorted us to the door. "I'm so sorry," she said, more to Norah than to me. "She's had a hard year at school, all on her own. It won't happen again."

"It better not," Norah said.

"She's going home in a couple of days. Is it still okay if I drop by?"

"Of course," said Norah more kindly. "But call first. And don't let her do anything like this again."

"I'll try. But you know, she's a big girl. I can't control her."

"If you can't, we'll have to charge her with kidnapping," said Norah.

She couldn't mean that, I thought. But I suspected already that she could be fierce.

At home, we found Vince and Kevin sitting on either side of my mother. Kevin was telling her about the latest triumphs of his Little League team. Tears came to my eyes seeing what good boys they were. Luz was still clutching me.

"What happened?" Vince asked. "Grandma said Sandra snatched her away and ran out."

"She's back now. Everything's okay," I said. "I'm glad you took good care of Grandma."

My mother held out her arms. "Come to Grandma, sweetie." But Luz refused to move from my arms, so I sat with her on my lap.

"Is it okay if we go upstairs?" Vince asked. "There's a big game on."

"Sure." Norah plopped into a chair with her head in her hands, and the boys left.

"What's this all about?" my mother began. "That girl Sandra must be ..." She looked over at Luz and stopped midway. "Well, is she?"

"Yes," Norah said.

"I always thought that adoption went too easily. I know people who've waited so long for a baby, and you both did it so fast. Are you sure it's all on the up and up?"

"It's completely legal," Norah said. "We have papers and everything. Our lawyer handled it. She wanted it. Sandra, I mean. She knew us. She trusted us. She didn't want a baby, she was a kid of seventeen."

Luz finally went over to my mother and nuzzled into her chest. She might even have fallen asleep.

"But what about the father?" said my relentless mother.

"We don't know, and she wouldn't tell."

"But what does it say on the birth certificate?" my mother persisted. I should be asking those questions. Whose name indeed? "If a father turns up, he could make trouble too."

I'd never even thought about the birth certificate. Had I ever seen it? I looked at Norah. She must know.

"I doubt that that could happen." Norah poured herself more coffee and bit into a muffin. "He's probably back in Mexico. I'm pretty sure he was deported—he wasn't here legally."

"Well, you should make sure."

"Look, Dorothy ... We've done everything properly. Sandra will go back to school in a couple of days. I mean, school must be out for spring break, but I think she has a part-time job too. She's studying nursing."

"Mom," I began, and waited for words to come. "Let me be straight with you about the accident. I had extensive memory loss—I don't remember any details about the adoption. At the beginning I didn't even remember ... where we lived, but thank goodness I've got all that back." That wasn't exactly being straight, but was as straight as I could manage. "The rest will come back gradually, the doctors said."

She shifted in her seat and rearranged Luz in her arms. "Well, what about me? And your father? Susan? Do you remember us?"

"Of course. It's more ... small details."

"I see. Well, you should get in touch with your sister. She's very concerned about you."

"I've been phoning her," said Norah. "She may even fly out for a visit. I'm not sure Monica will come. Susan says the Cooper Hewitt Museum is interested in some of her work, but they want to see the stuff, not just online. So Susan may bring it."

Susan on the way? Lugging pottery? News to me! Was this true, and had Norah forgotten to mention it? What other unexpected visitors could be knocking at the door?

Norah stood up. "I think I'd better put Luz to bed for a real nap. She must be exhausted." My mother handed her over. Luz opened her eyes for a moment— gray eyes like my mother's—then fell back asleep.

When they'd gone, my mother gazed at me sternly. I'd expected sympathy from my semi-confession. "Is there anything else you're not telling me?" she asked, as she stood up. Again she reminded me of my wife. I've heard that women marry people like their fathers, but never the opposite. I didn't know much about Norah's father, only that he drank after her brother was killed. But not on the truck. Her parents were gone, she'd said.

"No. Nothing that I remember," I tried to joke. "Oh, next week I'm going to a rehearsal. There was a new script waiting for me when I got home. I've almost got the whole thing down. No trouble with memory there. Just some more work tonight and tomorrow. It's about a suspicious husband."

"I'll look forward to that. And so will your grandmother. I'll be off now. It was good to see the kids."

"I'd drive you to the station, but I don't remember where the car is." I was appealing for sympathy and regretted it immediately. "I can call a cab."

"The car should be the least of your worries," she said. "Anyway, I have my own car."

"Norah said you didn't like driving in the city."

"I don't. But this was a special occasion, wasn't it? To see my only son who could have been killed?" I thought she brushed a tear from her eye, but maybe it was only a spot of dust.

When she was gone I lay down on the couch and tried to sleep. Was this ordinary family life? How eventful! I was more accustomed to blankness. How did people stand it?

"THAT GIRL SANDRA SEEMS DANGEROUSLY unhinged," I said in bed that night. "How come we trusted her with the boys?"

"She never acted weird before. She was a good babysitter. And she agreed easily enough to the adoption. She was seventeen, she didn't want a baby."

"She seemed to want her now."

"Well, it's almost five years later. She must have

changed her mind, grown up a bit. Anyway, I hope we've seen the last of her."

"Right. So where were we, with our bedtime stories?"

"I don't remember. Maybe we could take a night off."

"This is important. The last thing you told me was that we were faithful for the most part. What does that mean?"

"Why is this something you need to know? It's better to forget some things. Consider yourself lucky that way. Maybe you could forget about the divorce, at least for a while. It gets me on edge. I feel like I'm on probation."

"Of course you're not. I'm not thinking about divorce. I forgot I ever thought of it. You forget it too."

"That's your specialty, not mine," she snapped.

Below the belt, that was. "I just want to hear about the 'faithful for the most part' part." Since we'd been so fine in bed last night, I felt I could use persuasion. I put a hand on her breast and caressed the nipple. "I'll make you feel very good if you tell me."

"Oh, please. This is no joke, Joe."

"Please yes or please no?"

"No."

I removed my hand. "Then you'd better tell me. You'll have to sooner or later, so get it over with. Don't worry, after last night I don't care what you did. I'm in a forgiving mood."

"Are you? Well, I don't know if you're ready for this, but okay." She hesitated.

"Is it awful?"

"I wouldn't say awful now. It has a happy ending. But it was awful at the time."

"Spit it out." I pinned her arms back and leaned over her. Not a memory, but I somehow knew it was an old joke. "I have you in my power."

"Ow, you're hurting me. Let go. I told you Luz was adopted."

"Sure."

"So now you've seen her mother. She's what they call a 'dreamer.' You know what that means?"

"Yes. They're waiting to become citizens."

"Right. Sandra was brought here by her aunt as a small child."

"Yes. She went to school in the neighborhood and was starting at NYU. Incidentally, I've got to go back to the library next week, they need me. You'll be on your own. Anyway, she was in the library often, and I got to know her. Turns out she lived right around here. I asked her if she was interested in a babysitting job, for Kevin. I needed someone to pick him up at nursery school, the previous girl had left. You got him sometimes, but your hours were always changing, rehearsals, auditions and all. And Vince was only ten, really too young to leave on his own. It all worked out fine."

Why was she telling me all this? My heart started to race again. I shouldn't have pushed her to tell. Something not good was coming. "Well, go on."

"All right, she got pregnant." A long pause. I knew before she spoke next. "Luz is yours."

Mostly it was like fireworks exploding in my head. But beyond the shock, odd as it felt, was delight that this beautiful child was mine. Sure, even if a stranger had fathered her, she was mine now. But somehow this felt different. Mine. It meant more to me than knowing the boys were mine, because there was no mystery about them. But this girl who held my hand and trusted me ... So two of my children were unplanned. Only Kevin ... I must ask Norah how we decided on a second child.

The fireworks died down, and the good feeling was immediately overcome by a tsunami of self-loathing.

Wait, had I really done that? The more I thought about it, the more it felt impossible. I couldn't have done it. I have no special yen for teenagers. Not now, anyway. Could I have been that sort of creep ... Who knows what kind of women I liked. Except for Norah. No, those things can't change with a bump on the head. I wasn't that bad. After all I was a guy who was willing to marry a woman I'd knocked up. Wasn't that good?

Well, in the unlikely event that it was true, it's not as if this girl was Lolita; she was seventeen years old. But no, I couldn't have done it. Maybe she started it, throwing herself at me. But why would some schoolgirl want me? We were both quiet for a while. Finally, I said, "No. I don't accept it. She was in what, high school? You know these kids are screwing all the time. The father could have been anyone. Did I ever do anything like that before?"

"You mean sleep with a teenager? I don't imagine so, but only you would know. I'm not the suspicious type. I never went around looking in your pockets."

"Are you absolutely sure? Maybe she's lying to protect some boyfriend. Or she wanted money?"

"What kind of idiot do you think I am, Joe? There were DNA tests. I can show you the papers if you don't believe me. There's no doubt. And no, she never asked for money."

"So I'm supposed to believe I'm the kind of man who would sleep with a babysitter half his age and get her pregnant?"

"I don't know what kind of man that is. I just know it's what you did. I don't know how it happened, and you probably don't remember. Or do you?"

"Of course not. I can't even imagine doing it." I paused. "It couldn't be rape, could it?"

"You're asking the wrong person, Joe. She said it just happened. Maybe she liked you. Maybe she came on to you. You're sexy. Maybe you liked her. What does Skellings always say on *Crime City*? All you need is motive and opportunity."

"But what was my motive?"

"Do you need to ask?" Norah shrugged. "You're a man with a dick. Isn't that enough motive?"

I hadn't heard that tone before. This was all part of getting to know my wife. Maybe she was the one who'd thought of divorce and suggested it to me? How would I ever know? Any lingering doubts now that she was my wife had vanished. "Was it once or … or did it go on?"

"Will you stop interrogating me? Maybe you should ask her. I wasn't there, was I? She could have gotten an abortion—I offered to help—but by the time she realized, it was too late and besides, she and her aunt are good Catholics, they don't believe in it. She's not a sophisticated girl. She didn't want a baby. She wanted to go to California and become a nurse. She was miserable over it. Her aunt was miserable. Sandra came here and had hysterics. You think it was a picnic for me?"

"I'm sorry." It was so inadequate. I didn't know what else to say.

"You're sorry now? You were sorry then too. But it doesn't help. I was ready to pack up and leave, but I couldn't do that to the boys. It was my idea to adopt the baby. I'd always wanted a girl so much, I told you, but I couldn't get pregnant again. I made her take a test to find out the sex. You didn't object, you were walking around with that silent hangdog look guilty men get. If it had been a boy, I don't know …"

"Why didn't you tell me all this before?"

"Maybe I should have. But things were going along well, you were getting used to your life … It wouldn't have made any difference, would it? I mean in how you felt about Luz. And there were so many ugly scenes. I didn't want to remember them. I thought I could tell you later. Who could imagine that Sandra would turn up and make another scene?"

The world was a dangerous place indeed. This didn't compare with mass murders. But it was mine. My disaster.

"But it didn't bother you that you thought she was … mine?"

"It wasn't just a thought. It was the truth. And it didn't bother me. I mean, the fact that you'd done it bothered me, sure. More than I can say—a babysitter, Joe, for fuck's sake. But as far as Luz, no. I liked that. At least she was partly ours. Yours. And right away there was no difference, she became mine too. As soon as I held her in my arms, there was no difference. I tried to get over my anger and patch things up. And we were getting Sandra out of a lot of trouble. The aunt was relieved. Sandra didn't even tell her family back in Oaxaca. And of course Rosa was glad there wouldn't be an abortion— she's a regular churchgoer. Anyway it was too late, as I told you. So it all worked out."

"And you arranged all this for me? To save my skin?"

"I wasn't concerned about your skin. I told you, it was more for me. It seemed the simple solution. And it did work out. Just look at her. Isn't she the most lovable child? And smart too."

I'm thinking it's all a hoax. I couldn't have done it. Not with a teenaged babysitter. It was just too … sordid. I didn't know if I'd been a faithful husband—I hoped so. But this was not even love, or anything remotely related to it. An impulse I couldn't resist? No, I couldn't let that be me. Yet there seemed no doubt that I did it. Luz was such a lovely child—I should be proud to claim her. Thank God Sandra and Rosa didn't believe in abortion.

"Well, I don't like this person you're saying I am. Did you love me after that?"

"I was very angry. I was furious. And disgusted. But I suppose I loved you. What does love mean after many years of living together? Who knows?"

"What about now?"

She looked up sharply. "How can I answer that? I loved the person who went out jogging that Monday. I loved the person who was in our bed last night. But sometimes you're like a stranger who came into our lives. I wouldn't ask you if you love me. It wouldn't be fair. What I think is, you thought of divorce because of how we got together. It wasn't romantic. And after I got pregnant, not even so passionate. That returned later."

"You said we fell in love."

"We did, but I think now that you wanted a different kind of love, not with a baby in the background getting up in the middle of the night. I think you wanted a drama. A great love, like something in a play or a book. I can almost understand. But is that a reason to disrupt the lives of three kids, a family ...?"

We were silent for a while. "Do the boys know, about Luz, I mean?" I asked.

"No, just that we adopted her and Sandra went away. Maybe someday they'll figure it out but for now, no."

How I longed for a pill, a shot, some magic potion that would make me know who I was, what I was. Good enough not to desert a woman carrying my child. Bad enough to fuck a teenaged babysitter. All at once it seemed unbearable, I wanted to die and be buried in an unmarked grave. Here lies no one.

A movie I'd seen the other night came back to me, a sleepless night when I pursued my amnesia research. Something about sunshine. Yes, *Eternal Sunshine of the Spotless Mind.* A young couple's affair starts going badly. The movie is disjointed, fragments of their times together, good and bad. He is saturnine, she is whimsical, opposites you wouldn't think would get together. They resort to a hokey scientific procedure that can erase all the memories of the one who's caused pain. If only Norah and I could sign up for a similar experiment. But no, I wouldn't want her expunged, of course not. When the two accidentally meet again after the procedure, strangers on a train, they are once again attracted and will start up again—showing that we make the same bad choices over and over. Still, if only Norah and I could start anew, I'd never do that again.

Norah stroked my shoulder. "Come on, Joe. It could be worse. Would you rather have cancer? Something you could die of?"

She was not diplomatic, I knew that already. And of course she was still angry. Having to tell the story all over … I shouldn't be surprised. Even Skellings wouldn't stoop to a teenager. However much she loved Luz, what wife wouldn't be furious. The profound banality of it sickened me. Why couldn't I have picked a grown woman, at least?

"I can understand that you're angry."

She gave a dry laugh. "You sound like a therapist. Do you know, you even thought of being a therapist at one point, when you weren't getting any roles. But then *Crime City* came along, and you got a long-term contract. Look, this is hard on all of us. We're all doing our best. And I'm hoping your memory will come back. It might take a couple of months, the doctor said."

"Did Sandra ever come to see her?"

"A couple of times when she was an infant. She really wasn't too interested. She was a very young, not terribly bright girl. She wanted to get away. As soon as she could, she transferred to a school in California where she could study nursing. I knew at some point she might face the fact that she had a daughter, but I thought it would take longer. I tried to forget she existed."

"What about her aunt?"

"She comes over now and then. You saw her, she's getting on, must be over sixty. But she's still in good shape. Luz calls her Tia Rosa. She's a kind old lady. She brings us treats, cakes and things. Sometimes she cooks for us, you know, Mexican dishes, and we all eat together."

"I suppose she's furious at me too."

"Well, you're not her favorite person, let's put it that way. Besides the affair with Sandra"—I winced at that word—"she blames you for her moving so far away. But she knows we're taking good care of Luz and bringing her up well, and she appreciates that—she couldn't manage it at her age. And she's glad we live so close. If she were adopted by other people ... So she tolerates you."

"Does she know about the accident?"

"Yes, she saw it in the paper. You know, in spite of all that's happened, she still watches your show religiously every week. I think she's tickled to know someone on TV."

And she rolled over with her back to me. No love tonight.

AGAIN THE LIMO TOOK ME TO THE STUDIO. Again I'd studied the names of the crew and my fellow actors—Norah described them so that I'd recognize them—and I made sure to find out the receptionist's name: Julie. I had a pretty good memory, I was pleased to discover. I remembered everything I'd learned in the past week and a half. A pity to lose such a good memory. But after learning about my episode with Sandra, I wasn't sure I wanted it to return. There might be more things I'd regret knowing. No, of course I wanted it to return. I couldn't continue this way forever. A blank past meant an incomprehensible present. I'd be seeing the doctor in a few days; I'd be patient.

I brought Julie a dozen roses and wrote her name on the card, so she'd forgive me for calling her "you" on my first visit. She was pleased and sent me on to the rehearsal area where a bunch of people were gathered. I found Jonathan, and we shook hands. It wasn't hard greeting the others, a half dozen or so, because they came crowding around to ask how I was and comment on my cane. They were a lively bunch, and I wondered which might be friends and which simply work acquaintances. In the background, men were noisily working on the set.

Jonathan introduced me to the guest star, a middle-aged paunchy man who was playing the wife's accountant, a shady type who assists her in moving money around unobtrusively. From the way they all treated him I understood he was a quite well-known actor, and I made an effort to be friendly; after all I was the main character, and we had a few short scenes together. To my surprise, he was the one who seemed pleased to meet me. I had no idea then of what kind of reputation I had, but his response made me think I was better known than I'd imagined.

Jonathan spoke for a while about the script and marked out guidelines on the floor with chalk. I can't say I remembered anything specific about the process, but it echoed in my head, like an elusive dream. I trusted that when we began I'd know what to do. And I did. There were two brief scenes in my office where the suspicious husband came to consult me. They went fine. All I had to do was act respectable and ask the usual questions that anyone who's seen a few detective movies could supply. In the next scene I met the wife in a hotel bar—she'd been in a couple of episodes before, and working with her felt familiar. The bar scene was not yet fully furnished, no bottles and only a table, but that would be taken care of by the time we shot the scene. I was supposed to act like a guy trying to pick her up, but she was savvy and immediately psyched out that I'd been hired by her husband. I didn't try to deny it. Jonathan didn't make too many comments; he only advised me to handle the cane more provocatively.

During the few scenes I wasn't in, I sat to one side and watched. "Anyone mind if I smoke?" I said.

"Joe, have you been on Mars?" Julie asked as she went around pouring coffee. "You always smoke here." So I did, and I wasn't alone. Perhaps this was the last place in New York where smoking was permitted. One of the women moved off and discreetly coughed, but I ignored her. I was the star, after all. Then I grasped that she was playing my on-and-off girlfriend, Cheryl. Later on we had to embrace, and Jonathan told her to put a little feeling into it. "Hotter," he said. "Remember, you're still hoping he'll ask you to move in with him."

"It's the smoke," she said. "Sorry, Joe."

"I'm sorry. I forgot how you feel about it." Someone gave me a mint, and we carried on with a bit more ardor.

After a while Julie sent out for sandwiches, and we all sat around and ate. The others gossiped about various shows, what would last and what wouldn't, and I listened carefully to keep up. They all knew I'd been in the hospital and then laid up with my ankle—I tried to make more of that than it truly was. Still, I hadn't been isolated from TV or the web. I needed to get on track. If only I had a friend here, I thought, someone I could be frank with and who could help me along. But even without a past, I knew this business instinctively; it wasn't a good idea to confide my vulnerabilities to anyone.

THE BOOK SAUL GAVE ME IS HYPNOTIC, mostly because the main character, Stiller, who is a sculptor, persists against all evidence in claiming he's not who he is. He languishes in prison entertaining his guard with fantastical stories about his adventures in Mexico, which may or not be real. When visitors come, he pretends not to know them. His wife, a dancer whom he seems to have abandoned in a tuberculosis clinic six years ago, comes to visit, and even that can't change his stubborn refusal, though they do seem to fall in love all over again. In time the cause of his stubbornness becomes clear. He hated his life, he hates everything about Switzerland, he hated his troubled marriage, and he hates his own work as well: at one point, brought to his studio, he destroys his sculptures. He simply doesn't want any part of who he is, rejects that identity entirely. He takes on a new name and spends years in the US and Mexico, or so he claims. Finally, near the end he is forced to admit that he is indeed Stiller, suggesting that we can't change who we are. Something I knew to begin with. Very clever, a very good read, a philosophical exploration of identity, blah blah blah. I even start jotting down some quotes. But by the time I get to the end I'm mad.

Why did Saul recommend it? Is he suggesting that I'm like Stiller, that I know perfectly well who I am, I haven't forgotten a thing, but I simply don't want to be Joe Marzino or live his life anymore? That's absurd. I've accepted this life; of all the possible lives I might have lived, this one isn't at all bad. Indications so far have convinced me that I'm Joe Marzino. Good enough. What is my "friend" trying to tell me?

So I call Saul. I'd rather email or text him, but I can't put all I want to say in an email.

A hearty greeting. I hear a clink, probably opening a can of beer with one hand. "Glad to hear from you, Joe. How're you getting on?"

"The same. Listen, I read that book you gave me. *Stiller?*"

"Aha. So what did you think?"

"As a novel, fine, great. But I'm bothered about why you gave it to me. Do you think I'm putting on some sort of act? Because I'm an actor? So they tell me, anyway."

"Not an act, man. But something, I don't know, maybe, could be willed in all this? Unconsciously, of course. Like, maybe you want a different life, and you've hit on this way to go about it?"

"How could I want a different life if I don't even remember my actual life, what you say I'm rejecting? And if my real life is what I'm leading now, or pretending to lead, it's not any different. For fuck's sake, you knew Norah from before, you know she's my wife. You've been to my house before. You're way off base. Stiller fled the country and made a new life. He didn't have trouble with memory loss. He was quite capable of starting all over elsewhere. I'm barely able to recognize my neighbors, much less continue my own life without Norah prompting me every other minute." I'd raised my voice. I was almost shouting.

"Hey, there's no need to get so angry. It was just a thought. I thought maybe reading about someone in your predicament might help you."

"But he's not in my predicament. That's what I'm trying to tell you. You think I'm hiding from something in my past that I want to forget? But I've already forgotten it."

"Okay, okay, maybe it was a mistake. I'm sorry if I offended you."

"What offends me is that you don't believe me. You think I'm putting on an act. What good would that do me?"

"People want to forget certain things. Repress them. You must know that."

I tried to calm myself. Best to get this over with. "Look, I suppose you meant well. Let's let it go."

"Fine with me," he said. "I'll be in touch. You up to a game of squash yet?"

"No. My ankle is still out of commission."

"When it's better, we'll have a game together."

"Righto," I said, and hung up.

THAT NIGHT, AS NORAH SAT READING BESIDE me, I made myself close Saul's book and call my sister back. It was about time I summoned the will or the nerve to speak to her. I had an inexplicable vague fear about her. Something had happened, that's all I sensed.

"She's very concerned," Norah said. "At least she

says so. Your mother is unhappy about Susan's being gay, and the horses. I don't know what she has against horses. I guess she expected something different, more … urban. Closer. She's unhappy that they live so far away, although if they were closer, it would be harder on all of them. Plus, she's not wild about Monica, who's built like a wrestler and speaks her mind. She's never said anything about her being Black. At least she's not a bigot. Or she just doesn't care."

"How do you feel about them?"

"Okay. I'm fine with your sister; she's a bit like you, easygoing, a light touch. I'm comfortable with her. But I find Monica a bit scary. I told you, she doesn't hesitate to say what she thinks about our life. It's not us personally, she says, but what we represent. White privilege. Oblivious to the rest of the world. And so on."

"Well, she has a point, doesn't she?" Unless my father was really a petty criminal. But even petty criminals lead bourgeois lives, don't they? "Will Susan have to stay here when she visits?" I asked.

"Not if I can help it. Your study has a fold-out bed, but you'd have to move things around. And the basement, which I don't think she'd like. We never really finished it. Though it does have a working bathroom. Anyway, I'll suggest the hotel a few blocks away. She might prefer that. We can foot the bill."

"That reminds me. I never asked you about money. I've hardly spent anything since the hospital. Do we have any?"

She laughed. "Do you mean our net worth? At the moment we don't need to worry. We were struggling along, and then came the financial crisis, but then you became Skellings, and that helped a lot. Also when my father died, he left us a pile. I can show you papers some time."

"I thought your parents didn't have anything. You've said you grew up poor."

"I did. But then my father started investing in Apple early on and did extremely well. And then he died before he could enjoy it. My mother died years ago too. My sisters and I divided everything up, and it came to more than I expected. But we can talk about money another time. Also I have a little job on the side I'll tell you about soon. Meanwhile, why don't you face the music and call Susan."

My sister's voice sounded familiar, a bit like my mother's, but younger. "Joe, I'm so glad you're okay. Norah told me about the accident. But look, this is not a good time to talk. We're on our way to visit some friends. Let me just tell you when my flight arrives …"

You would never know from our talk that we were once close. Twins, sharing a tight space. But maybe I was oversensitive. Besides being vaguely afraid of her. She'd take a cab from the airport, she said, so I needn't do anything. And she already had a hotel reservation. Oh, and Monica couldn't make it. She was sorry but had to prepare for a show at a local gallery.

I had expected more, much more. More feeling, more investment … a twin, after all. But Norah reminded me that even before the accident, I only saw her every year or so. After I hung up, disappointed and vaguely uneasy, Norah showed me an unusual set of mugs Monica gave us last Christmas. They were blood-red with streaks of green and blue, large, with big handles. They gave the impression of someone bold and forthright, with no doubts about her identity, if you can tell anything from a mug, that is. I have no idea what my sister is like, but from Norah's imaginings, something had happened between us. Could that be the missing piece? As children we must have been close, twins after all. Or was I making stupid assumptions again? Trying and failing to remember is exhausting. Playing a role for which I haven't read the script, for which there is no script, is exhausting.

I hope I wasn't mean to Susan about her being gay—after all, a teenaged boy in the suburbs with a gay sister. I don't imagine I was, that was never one of my prejudices, at least as far as I knew. But if she flaunted it, if she was butch, stocky, with raggedy hair and baggy jeans, I might have been embarrassed in school … God, who the hell was I?

There I am not thinking about sex at all, rather worrying about what I would say to Susan when she appears, when Norah turns around in bed and murmurs something. She puts her hand on my cock. "How are you feeling tonight?"

It's the first time she's approached me, and I don't want to waste it. Even in my present state I know sex is a great distraction. I take off her nightgown and touch her everywhere, her breasts, her ass, and when I get my hand between her legs and start fingering her slowly, outside and in, she begins moaning and comes in two minutes.

"Hot chick," I say.

"I was thinking about this all the time you were reading. What are you reading that's so absorbing?"

"A book Saul gave me. I'll tell you later." I climb on top of her and get inside. "I'm going to make you come all night."

This goes on, not all night, but for a long time. We're moaning and gasping like newlyweds. It's as if we're making up for lost time. I may not know who I am, but I certainly know how to do this; it's not memory, it's something else. We're who we used to be, even if I can't remember that. I push hard, and she comes again, me too. I turn her over, and again. On it goes. I'm impressed with myself. Relieved that we can be this way. Why would I ever have wanted a divorce with someone like this in my bed? A stupid question. Even I remembered that sex is just a fleeting answer to any problem.

Finally we're exhausted and lie side by side, holding hands. "Is this how it used to be?" I ask.

"Sometimes," she murmurs. "Once in a while. When you fuck it's you again."

THINGS ARE BUSY IN *CRIME CITY*. AFTER WE polished off the script about the suspicious husband, we started a new one about a serial killer who preys on old women, a sort of latter-day Raskolnikov. Skellings was especially hard on him, he had to be restrained by the cops from beating him to a pulp; he obviously has a soft spot for old women as well as children.

Rather than take the limo again on my next trip, I ventured on the subway. I studied the route beforehand—this was my first real expedition without Norah, like a first-grader who's allowed to walk to school by himself. To my surprise I remembered all the subway stops and found my way to the studio easily. Could it be my memory returning? No, simply the retention of ordinary knowledge, I forget what they called it on the websites. I'd been riding these subways for years. One good thing about carrying the cane—I got a seat immediately, a middle-aged Black woman in jeans and a t-shirt that said *Be the Dream*. As soon as she noticed me, she stood and waved me over.

Jonathan wanted a quick first read of the next script, the one after Raskolnikov. I was dreading that. When I first read it at home, the story made me edgy. A group of drunk teenaged boys get into an accident driving late at night, coming home from a party, and hit a cyclist. Halfway through my heart started fluttering. No wonder it was disturbing—I had sons and could imagine them in that predicament. Though Vince didn't even have his learner's permit yet. I even dreamed about it that night and woke up in a sweat. I went downstairs so as not to wake Norah and worked on a crossword puzzle.

The actors playing the three boys—none of them teenagers themselves, of course—arrived late, and I was tired. They were energetic and very convincing. Maybe because I didn't like the script and it'd been a long afternoon, they irritated me, and I did something an experienced actor should never do: I let my annoyance bleed into the lines, and Skellings showed his anger before he finished hearing their version. I almost swatted one around, the swaggering one, but stopped myself in time. I don't know what came over me.

"Hey, hey," Jonathan intervened. "Take it easy, Joe. That's not in the script. Skellings is supposed to be cool. Threatening, but not violent."

"Sorry," I said. "Can we go over that again?"

"We'll have to." The actor I'd almost hit was glaring at me.

"I'm really sorry, Perry. I just lost myself for a moment."

"Never mind," he mumbled. "We all have our off days."

I finished the scene well enough and was relieved as the ending neared and the police took over. As far as I knew, this had never happened to me before. It was a beginner's error. I apologized again, and before I left, I tossed cold water on my face and studied that face in the bathroom mirror as if it might tell me something, but as usual it revealed nothing. I hailed a taxi to get home. I still didn't know where the hell our car was parked, I thought angrily. Why hadn't Norah told me yet? At least she'd told me we had a car.

LATE ONE EVENING, AFTER TEN, THE PHONE rings. "Would you get it?" Norah asks from the couch in the living room. "I'm so tired."

I answer with trepidation. I haven't gotten in touch with any friends yet, can't even remember who they are. Except Saul. Or it could be my mother.

"Good evening, Mr. Marzino," says the female voice on the other end. "I hope it's not too late to call. This is Clara Keller, upstairs in 5B?" She sounds elderly but has already adopted the rising inflection of the young. Are you sure about that? I'm tempted to ask. "I hope you're feeling better after your accident. What an awful thing."

"I'm doing better, thank you. It's a slow process, but yes. So what can I do for you, Ms. Keller?"

"It's those two men downstairs in 4B, the ones who have the balcony?"

"Yes?"

"Well, now that the weather is warmer, it's the same goings-on as last fall."

"And that was?" I ask.

"I can't believe you don't remember, Mr. Marzino. We had several talks about it. You said you'd look into it, and then the weather got colder, so they weren't out anymore and so ... But now it's spring and as I told you more than once, I can see them from my kitchen window, right above the balcony ..."

"Ms. Keller, I think I'd better let my wife handle this. I'm not completely caught up with building matters yet." Before she can answer, I hand the phone to Norah, right beside me on the couch, reading a magazine. I cover the mouthpiece with my hand.

"Clara Keller," I whisper, but of course she already knows. "What's this all about?"

Norah frowns and takes the phone. "How are you, Clara? I hope everything's okay upstairs."

"Yes, but as I was just telling your husband, it's those two men in 4B just below me? That mixed couple."

Norah turns on the speaker so I can follow this better. "Kenneth and Frank, you mean? They're such nice guys, and quiet, as you know. What's the problem?"

Clara Keller's voice booms into the night. "Norah, you know very well what the problem is. I talked to your husband about it last fall. They lie out there on their chaise lounges with their drinks and the Sunday papers and ... well, they hold hands and sort of play games with their feet and well, even kiss. It isn't decent. It's a public space. I can't comment on what they do in private, but I shouldn't have to witness that from my kitchen window."

I move away a few inches so I can laugh quietly. Norah is covering her mouth to suppress her giggles.

"Clara, as Joe explained to you last fall, it isn't a public space. It's their private balcony. And what they're doing doesn't sound like ..."

"It may be a private balcony, but I can see right into it from my kitchen window while I'm cooking. I shouldn't have to see that kind of thing in my own home even if it's accepted now. And that Kenneth is the only Black person in the building."

"Tell her I'll find another next time an apartment is vacant," I whispered to Nora.

"What does that mean?" Norah asked.

"Well, you'd think he'd make an extra effort to behave properly."

"So what do you suggest we do, Clara? We can't tell them not to use the balcony."

"You could have a word with them. Tell them their antics are disturbing the other tenants …"

"It's not the other tenants, Clara. It's just you."

"Tell her not to look out the window," I murmured to Norah, but she pushed me away.

"Your husband said he'd have a word with them last year, but it doesn't seem to have helped."

"Did you?" Norah whispered as she covered the mouthpiece of the phone. "Have a word with them?"

"I wouldn't know."

"Or you could just ask them to leave because they're disturbing the other tenants," Ms. Keller said.

"Oh, I don't think we could do that. It's not even legal, and even if it was … We can't control their behavior. It's not like it's anything indecent or …"

"Indecent is a matter of opinion. My brother is a lawyer, and I'm going to consult him."

"Oh, Clara, is that really necessary? It'll make a lot of hard feelings, and it's not anything you can take to court. As your brother will certainly tell you. Why don't you just try to ignore it? You know, live and let live."

"Ignore it, you say? Well, I've been here six years, and they just moved in two years ago, and I never thought you'd treat me like this. Are you going to force me to move and leave those … types there?"

"Clara, please, no one is suggesting you move. We've always gotten along. Let's not make an issue of this."

But she had hung up. To Clara Keller, too, the world was a dangerous place, even in her kitchen.

Now we could laugh freely. "But it's not really so funny," Norah said.

"Why not?"

"She could make trouble. Speak to other tenants. She could make things unpleasant. Did you really say you'd have a word with them?"

"How would I know?" I responded. "If she says so, I suppose I did. But I couldn't have meant it."

"We're friendly with them, Ken and Frank. They've come down a couple of times for a glass of wine. They've called to ask about you, but I haven't invited them down yet, I wanted to give you some more time."

"If we're friendly, maybe we could have a word with them. You could. You're more diplomatic. Tell them not to play with their feet." I nudged her bare foot with my own.

"Oh, come on, Joe, I'd never …"

"Do you think she'd actually leave, if it came to that?" I asked. "Maybe that wouldn't be so bad."

"A woman in her seventies living on Social Security. Where could she go?"

"Maybe a convent?" I suggested.

"It's not funny. You know what rents are like. Or maybe you don't. Everything is sky high nowadays."

"Then she'll have to get used to it."

"This is all going to end up in my lap," Norah grunted. "Like so many things."

A disgruntled wife. Unlike her. "Then I'll handle it the next time she complains. Let's go to bed."

"I want to finish this article. It's barely eleven o'clock."

"I didn't mean sleep. We could hold hands or play

games with our feet."

"Very funny." But she put the magazine aside to join me. At the foot of the stairs I stepped aside chivalrously so she could precede me, and I could watch the undulations of her ass as she moved, I suppose all men like to follow women up stairs for that reason. Though I don't remember ever discussing it.

"NOTHING?" SUSAN WAS INCREDULOUS.

"Nothing."

"Do you mean not even the accident?" my sister asked. She was leaning back in the armchair, her legs crossed, relaxed, with a drink in her hand. Every now and then she shook it, and the ice cubes rattled around. She had arrived last night and checked into a nearby hotel. This was the first time I'd seen her in who knows how long. The kids were in school, the house was quiet. I was filled with dread, the kind of dread you feel when you're young and applying for a job or at a college interview. It was absurd. This was my sister, we had shared months in a womb. Grown up together.

She was nothing like what I'd imagined. I had expected a horsy type, maybe a whiff of the stables. But she was wearing some floral scent—I suddenly remembered that about our mother—she always wore perfume. My twin sister was large-boned and slim, elegantly dressed, like our mother, a cream-colored silk shirt and designer jeans with high black boots. I tried to see signs of me in her face but didn't find any. Well, we were fraternal twins. Her hair, though—it was dark and coarse like mine. She had it drawn back from her face and tied in a ponytail that fell over her shoulder. Her skin was just a tad darker than mine, maybe that was the outdoors, the horses, Wyoming, Colorado, one of those square states marked off by a ruler. Her eyes were very unusual, an almost emerald green. But maybe they were contacts; I knew from TV that eyes could be made just about any color.

"What accident? I told you I don't remember anything."

"But that ... That was something I thought you couldn't possibly forget."

"Well ..." I waited.

She waited too, reluctant. "Okay, it was the graduation party when we were through with high school. The party isn't important except that you and your two idiot friends, Frank Winston and Danny Nuzzo, got totally plastered. You honestly don't remember?"

I shook my head. How bad could this be? She was up and about, I hadn't injured her permanently.

"You were driving. You were maybe the least drunk but still pretty sloshed. You hit a guy on a bicycle and kept going."

But I had been hit by a guy on a bicycle, hadn't I? I didn't remember that either.

"You mean we just left him there?"

"You would have. But I said we had to go back and see if he was okay. Call the cops. Something. You wouldn't give in. I put my foot on the brake and leaned over you and grabbed the wheel. Luckily, there were no other cars on the road. I turned the car around and went back, it was only, oh, I guess a couple of hundred feet. The guy was lying perfectly still, I was so scared, I thought you'd killed him. I got out of the car and called the cops. Your friends tried to stop me. You were in a fog, sort of like you are now actually."

"Was he dead?"

"No, the cops got him up. They were afraid his neck

was broken, but it wasn't. It turned out to be his hip. He was in a wheelchair for a couple of months. But that was later. Meanwhile I was scared shitless that we'd killed someone. That you'd killed someone. But before the cops arrived, your friends had some advice for you." She stopped and her face flushed. After all this time. It must get worse.

"What?"

"You had gotten a scholarship to Harvard. Because you were so smart, you know?" She gave a small bitter smile. "You were the smart one."

"I'm sorry." Must I apologize for being smart? "Weren't you smart too?"

"You were the one people bragged about. Such a bright boy, everyone said. Such prospects. So your friends decided you might lose the scholarship to Harvard, not to mention the rest of your entire future life, if you'd been caught driving drunk and killed someone."

"But it was an accident. And he wasn't dead, you said."

"We didn't know that yet. Anyway, no one was in their right mind. Your friends said I had to say I was driving, and of course my fingerprints would be on the wheel because I grabbed it from you. So that's how it went down. The cops asked who was driving—we were all out of the car by then—and everyone said it was me."

"And I let them do that?"

"You went along with it. Like you sort of forgot I was your sister. Right after that, the cops got the fellow conscious, slapped his face around, he was a middle-aged guy, just blacked out, hadn't the faintest idea what happened."

Like me. I hadn't the faintest idea what happened. Could this be what nagged at me? The missing piece?

"Did he even remember his name?"

"Oh sure, he knew everything. Not like what happened to you. He was just complaining of the pain in his side and wanted to call his wife. An ambulance came. That was a relief."

"But we all said you were driving?"

"Well, they said. You said. I didn't say much. I must have been in shock. And I was furious at you for being so drunk. I wasn't drunk, I never drank much, so you all figured I was safe, I couldn't get charged with anything. Not that we were legal scholars or anything, but at least we knew drunk driving was serious."

"Weren't you going to college? Harvard too?"

"No, I was tired of being in the shadow of my smart brother. Smart, good looking, the works. I was going far away, to Reed, in Oregon. I had no trouble about the accident, except of course guilt. Which I'm not even sure you had. It was simply called an accident, and Dad and the insurance handled everything. They were furious with me, of course."

"With you? You mean they didn't know?"

"They didn't know. Your sterling reputation was safe, Joe. Mom still doesn't know."

"Oh my God. I'm so sorry."

Susan looked up into the distance as if she were remembering. "It's a little late for that isn't it? You barely said a word about it afterwards. I was just coming out. I had a girlfriend. I was skinny and bony and wore colorless t-shirts without a bra and had my hair cut short. I was the gay sister you weren't so happy about. Neither were our parents. You probably don't remember, but we didn't, let's say, keep in close touch after that."

"All these years?"

"Well, we saw each other now and then. It was

unavoidable. But it wasn't like before, I mean when we were kids. Twins, you know."

"We were close, before?"

"Very."

"I am so sorry. What can I say? I was a stupid kid."

"You absolutely were. But you know the worst thing about it, I mean aside from that poor guy being in a wheelchair and having two operations on his hip? The worst thing was that you never even thanked me. I took the rap, as they'd say on that stupid cop show that provides you with …" she waved her hand at the room, the furniture, the windows, everything. "All this." She smiled again, this time with genuine amusement, and I wanted to smile with her, but how could I?

"Do you watch that?"

"Sometimes. With Monica. When we want a few laughs, or, to tell the truth, when I feel like seeing you. You're pretty good, the role suits you."

"That's not what Norah thinks. She says I'm nothing like Skellings. That's why I can do him so well, it's not method acting, believe me. The kids wish I were more like him. But that's not important. Of course I should have thanked you. I mean, I shouldn't have let you take the blame in the first place. I feel terrible about it. I probably owe the rest of my life to you."

"Well, I wouldn't go quite that far," Susan said in an ironic tone that reminded me of Norah. "But yes, you certainly owed me a thank you. Maybe even a little gift, like, oh, I don't know, a horse or something." She laughed.

"Pick out a horse, and I'll buy it for you. I don't know how to buy a horse."

"Joe, I was kidding. You used to have a sense of humor."

"Thank you," I said. "It's very belated, but thank you." I had the impulse to walk over and hug her, but I resisted. Was I impulsive that way in my real life? The appalling story Susan had just told me merited some impulsive affection. And I felt it. Or I should say I felt the gratitude and the guilt, so terribly belated. But it was clear she didn't want to be close, simply tolerated me in some primitive family way. Or was tied to me by things we'd been through together that my drastically reduced self had lost entirely. Our father's death, for one. God knows what else. Did she know my kids? Did I call her when they were born? Did she care?

She had to care; we were twins, we had huddled together for nine months. She might not like me in the least, but there's a closeness that has nothing to do with liking. She knew me, and she cared. She was close enough and distant enough that I could tell her the dream I had a few nights ago, about sitting on the floor of a small plane with other passengers, and we were slowly going down, so slowly that I hoped we might just bump on the tarmac and pick up our luggage and all go home, even though I knew that was almost impossible. I hadn't been able to tell Norah about it—it was right after we made love, I didn't want to spoil that night, or maybe I didn't want to frighten her; she was frightened enough of my amnesia.

"So what do you make of that?" I asked. "Does it mean I'm afraid I'll die without remembering? Or a death wish?"

"Well, I'm no dream expert. It could mean anything, but what it reminds me of is 9/11."

"9/11? Oh shit, I forgot all about that."

When she looked puzzled I said, "I don't mean forgot the way I forgot my whole life, just forgot like ordinary people forget. Of course I remember. It was terrible.

It was what, a dozen years ago? Kevin wasn't born yet. Vince must have been in kindergarten or first grade. Mostly I remember seeing it on TV over and over, who knows, maybe what I remember is from TV …"

"Pop was on his way out the door when he heard it on the radio. He never went out that day. And Mom was terrified. She must have called me half a dozen times. I was still living in New York back then."

"So you think it was that? But why would I dream about it now?"

"How would I know, Joe? Uncle Barry died, do you remember that?"

"No." I shook my head, with a sick feeling in my gut. I wanted to remember Uncle Barry and was too ashamed to say I didn't.

"Mom was frantic. Well of course, everyone was. He worked in a bank on one of the top floors and was one of those people who jumped out a window. I'm sure she'll be telling you about it. She likes to relive that day. I don't mean likes, of course. I mean it stuck so vividly in her mind, whenever the subject comes up, she goes through it all again. They were close when she was growing up, and she never liked his wife. Jealous, I think—he was the big brother who was devoted to her. Well, enough of that. I think I'll head back."

"No, stay. The kids'll be home soon, and Norah. We'll have dinner. I want my kids to know you."

MOST PEOPLE'S LIVES ARE MADE OF THE stories they tell themselves. Such as that character Stiller in the book Saul gave me. My life now is made of the stories people tell me, Susan, Norah, and besides the death of her brother, surely my mother has more in store. Together, they are creating a character, not even as well-rounded as Skellings. A character I'm not sure I like, in fact I'm pretty sure I don't like. And must I accept that is the man I am? I don't accept it. I suppose I'm more like Stiller than I imagined. But he went off to start a new life, and here I am in the old one.

THAT NIGHT, I ASKED NORAH, "REMEMBER 9/11?"

"Remember? How could I forget? How could anyone? Did you just remember?"

"Susan reminded me. We talked about it a bit. She told me about my Uncle Barry. I don't remember him though."

"That was a gruesome end. Your mother can recite the story to this day. Everyone remembers where they were and what they did. I rushed out of the library with the others, staff, students. I could see the smoke pouring over from the west. We were coughing. My first thought was to get uptown to pick up Vince in school. But I was afraid to get on the subway, I was afraid I'd be stuck down there, so I started walking. The phone lines were tied up, but finally I was able to reach you. So you picked him up. After about a mile I caught a bus; it was packed."

What a lot I was missing. I was wishing I had been there. But of course I was there, I'd just lost the day. "Besides Barry, did we know anyone?"

"Well, there was the super's daughter from the big building on our corner. You'd know him. She was there for a job interview for one of the finance companies. And the wife of one of our professors. She was going to a dentist appointment in the neighborhood, and she'd never been inside the building, so she just went to have a look. And you know my friend Paula, from my book group? Her brother was a fireman. He never came out. There were others."

"But no one else really close to us?"

"No, but why do you keep asking?"

"Because I sometimes get this sick feeling. Something bad, or someone. Maybe it's about my uncle. I don't know. Like a sense of loss. Did they ever get Bin Laden?"

"Oh, you remember him? Yes, about two years ago. He was found hiding somewhere, and they killed him. A kind of derring-do capture. You were very interested, you read all about it and watched the news. You even joked that Skellings would have been a good man for the job."

"Did I? Make jokes about it?"

"Well, you always had a mordant sense of humor. You can google it if you're curious."

NORAH HAD GONE BACK TO WORK, SO I WAS picking up Luz at preschool most days. When I had a rehearsal, she arranged for a play date with a friend. Norah came with me the first time and made a point of greeting the other parents—mostly mothers—and babysitters by name so I wouldn't seem so out of it. I'm a quick study, from all those scripts I suppose, so I learned the names easily. It was harder to match the kids with the mothers, but Luz was excited to help me with that. "Rima isn't Katie's mother, she's Kyle's mother. Katie's mother is Vicki."

"Right, thanks for helping," I answered. "I just forgot for a moment. And who's coming over to play this afternoon?"

"Becky! I just told you before. Daddy, you forget everything."

"I know. I'll try harder."

I was a bit late on the third afternoon; by then my ankle was getting better, and I was used to climbing over the fallen chairs. Sally, the teacher, insisted that the toys be put away before they all left, which was a good thing because I could injure my other ankle tripping over them. Nearly all the kids had been collected. I found Luz clinging to Sally's jeans, whimpering, and standing over her was Sandra. I hadn't seen her since the day she tried to run off with Luz. I'd almost forgotten about her. Shouldn't she be back in California by now? When she saw me, Luz let go of Sally and darted over. I picked her up. "It's all right, it's all right, I'm here. What's going on?"

"I'm sorry, Joe," said Sally, who looked near tears herself. "I'm so glad you're here. This young lady"—she nodded towards Sandra—"is insisting she's Luz's mother and wants to take her home. I couldn't get her to—"

"But I am her mother," Sandra shrieked. The few remaining kids looked about, frightened.

"Of course she's not. You've known Norah for two years. How could she be Luz's mother?" To Sandra I said, "Please, don't make more of a scene. Please just go home now."

Luz had her arms around my neck and clung tightly.

"You can stop crying. I'm taking you home."

"He's my daddy," she said between gasps. "And she is not my mommy." Luz shook her head and wiped her nose on my shirtsleeve.

"I know that, honey," said Sally. And to Sandra, "I'm sorry, but I have to insist that you leave. You're getting the children upset."

"But I am her mother. I can prove it."

"Sandra," I said. "Let's walk out together. I'll walk you home, and you can calm down."

"And this is her father!" Sandra cried, pointing, almost jabbing at me.

"Yes, we know that," said Sally.

"It's all a mix-up," I said to Sally. "Sandra was our babysitter years ago. She's just a little confused now. Come, Luz. Do you have all your things?"

"I told you we leave everything in our cubbies, remember? All I need is my sweater and my lunchbox."

But she wouldn't get down, so Sally fetched her sweater and her *Simpsons* lunchbox and led us to the door. Sandra followed, but when we got outside, she didn't walk with us. As she hurried away, she turned and said, "It didn't work this time, but I'm not through with you yet. You haven't seen the last of me. I've contacted a lawyer."

"Nothing will change the situation. It's best if you just drop it. Once you're back to yourself maybe we can arrange a visit."

She stalked off, long angry strides. She was a rather tall girl, I noticed, then made myself stop noticing. It was more than a block before Luz allowed me to put her down, and by the time we got home, she was telling me about a video they'd seen about camels. "In the hot desert they ride on camels. And do you know they wear those long white robes to keep cool? I thought they would be hot, but it keeps them cool."

I was in a sweat myself, and after I gave her some milk and cookies, I opened a can of beer. I reminded her to go to the bathroom as Norah had instructed me, then we turned on the TV and watched some cartoons.

Before long she was drowsing with her head in my lap.

Kevin came home from school and tossed his backpack on the floor. "What's with her?"

"Nothing really. Something upsetting happened at school with one of the kids, a tantrum or something. How was your day?"

"Boring, as usual. But we're starting auditions for next year's orchestra so I've got to practice."

"You were in it all this year, weren't you?"

"Yeah, but they like to give different people turns. But I'm still the best, so they have to take me. I'm not too worried."

He disappeared into the kitchen, and I heard him rummaging in the refrigerator.

IT WAS MORE THAN A WEEK SINCE I'D LEFT the hospital, and I was overdue for a checkup. I had actually forgotten about the appointment. Not amnesia, just an ordinary act of forgetting. Could happen to anyone. Almost reassuring.

Norah reminded me. She keeps a calendar stuck on the fridge with magnets—some of them are funny sayings, and some are famous paintings. I recognized some of the paintings—prior knowledge. Thank you, Professor …? I'd lost his name but had a shadowy image of sitting in the dark listening to his lectures while the slides shifted every few minutes. There was a snatch of memory, but it led nowhere. Norah keeps track of everyone's comings and goings, Little League, preschool birthday parties, PTA meetings. So efficient. I keep track of rehearsals on my phone—I've never missed one.

Checking in at the hospital was cumbersome. And

I had total recall—every moment of my time there. Being wheeled out of the ambulance, the jumbled noises of the ER, the constant back and forth of rushing feet, the group of doctors around me with name tags. I was the only one without a name tag. I remembered the MRI machine, the white coffin with the hammering inside. I hardly minded backing into it again. The technician, a new one, or at least one I didn't recognize, said he'd get the results to the doctor right away, so we wouldn't have to wait.

The doctor was a red-faced balding man about sixty, with thick round glasses and a white coat, and he fiddled with a ballpoint pen, clicking the point in and out as he sat at his desk gazing at his computer. There were photos arrayed, facing us, three blonde girls smiling shyly at the camera. Also facing us was a small grayish figurine representing a human brain. While the doctor's eyes stayed fixed on the computer in the usual trance-like way, I studied the brain's folds and crannies. It was like a moonscape. Crevices and lumps, rather ugly, it seemed to me. I wouldn't want to spend my life studying it, but then I'd never been good at science in school. (Another bit of memory! How did I know that?) One of these days I'd have to study the parts of the brain more closely. The diagrams on the websites had made my head swim. I looked at the lumps and folds on the plastic brain and wondered in which of them my history was stored.

"Sorry to keep you waiting," he said, after clearing his throat. "I'm afraid I don't have any good news for you." He paused. "On the other hand nothing really bad either. Nothing new has occurred, no bleeding or lesions, so you're no worse off than when you left, what is it, almost a couple of weeks ago? The thing is, there's no significant change. Which means ... The longer you go without your memory returning, the less likely it is to return. That is, parts will certainly return, they almost always do, but maybe not everything. We'll have to wait and see."

"Does that mean …?" I began. I wasn't sure what I intended to ask.

"I can't say anything definite. There have been cases of memory returning after months. As I said, the longer you continue without remembering, the less chance of a complete restoration. More likely partial. There's no way of knowing what parts will return. You have a lot of general memory, from what you've told me. You know facts about the world, which is a good sign. And you're … hold on"—he clicked on the computer and peered for a moment—"an actor. You said you're able to memorize the scripts you need for your work. The best I can tell you is to continue as you are—you seem to be functioning well, from what you said—and keep hoping. And come back in two weeks."

"So in other words I'm waiting for a miracle," I said.

"Not quite a miracle. But a change."

Norah and I were silent for a couple of minutes.

"We were hoping for better news," she said finally.

"I'm sure you were," he said and took off his glasses. His eyes were small and black like marbles. "I wish I had better news for you. But try to be grateful for what you have. You're in good health otherwise and have gotten adjusted to your life. You have a pretty good life, from what I gather. It could have been much worse. Serious brain damage is not a pretty thing. You only have damage in the—"

"So that's it," I said and started to get up.

"Make an appointment for two weeks from now on your way out, and keep up what you're doing."

We were silent in the elevator and on the bus home. We barely looked at each other, but Norah took my hand and held on to it.

I HOPED THAT I'D SEEN THE LAST OF SANDRA, but no. She kept turning up. What about nursing school in California? How could she take so much time off? Was it still spring break? Would she ever go back? A couple of times I saw her around the corner from the preschool, sitting at an outside table at a pizzeria studying her phone. Lurking. Waiting to pounce. I didn't know what she was capable of, how crazy she was. I made sure to get there early, and on the days I had rehearsals, Norah left work early. We didn't trust any babysitters.

Our lawyer, Howard Crane, called to say he'd been getting calls from a person saying she was Sandra's attorney, requesting a meeting. This made me seriously jittery, but Norah assured me it would come to nothing. Our papers were perfectly in order; Howard had gone over them many times. I dreaded this meeting, which would take place in his office. "A total waste of time," he'd called it, "but if you're willing to pay for the time, we'll do it."

Howard had been our lawyer for a long time, Norah reminded me. He helped us buy the house years ago, and he helped with the adoption. He could have helped us to sue the owner of the pizzeria whose delivery man had been killed in the accident that took my past, but I'd had no appetite for that. "You may be entitled to money," he urged, but I could only think of that poor dead guy with the pizza slices strewn around him and the kids snatching them.

The day before the meeting was scheduled, I spied

Sandra sitting at the pizzeria as Luz and I passed on the way home. It was drizzling, but she was under an awning and looked up from her phone as if she sensed we were nearby. I glanced over and nodded, but Sandra waved me towards her. Luz was afraid. She remembered the time Sandra had dragged her out of our house, as well as the time, recently, when she'd tried to pick her up at preschool. She didn't want to go over, but I held her in my arms and reassured her.

"She won't bother you, I've got you tight. She's just a young girl, a little mixed up."

"She wants to take me away."

"No one can take you away. We'll just say hello, we don't want to be rude."

Sandra motioned me to a chair and asked if I wanted a slice. She even offered one to Luz, who I could see was tempted, but shook her head, no.

"So did you hear from your lawyer?"

"Yes. We'll be there. But it's a waste of everyone's time. The papers are totally in order."

"Haven't you heard of cases where the decision is overturned?"

"Years ago, there was a big case involving a surrogate mother, a woman who'd carried someone else's baby and then changed her mind about giving it up. It has nothing whatsoever to do with our situation." How this old story came to mind I don't know. Part of the general knowledge the doctors talked about. "Ours is a legal adoption."

"I was underage when I signed."

"Your aunt signed with you, as your guardian. Is this what you called me over to talk about? Because I'm sorry, Sandra, I can't discuss it."

"That's not how you acted when... when, you know... Don't you remember? I remember you liked me then."

"Let me tell you something. I honestly don't remember. Not that I would forget, you're an attractive young woman." I could hardly bear to hear these platitudes coming out of my mouth. "I had this accident, you know? I was thrown off my bike. I have amnesia. I can't remember anything."

"You remembered those cases about the surrogate mothers."

"Yes, I know it's odd. I mean since the accident I can't remember about my past. I know I'm Luz's father because Norah told me. And I've seen the adoption papers. And the DNA results. And because Norah and I have raised her so far. But how it happened, between us, I don't remember."

She laughed harshly. "And you expect me to believe that?"

"It's the truth. Believe me, I wish I knew how it came about."

"How it came about? That's a laugh."

"Well, tell me, then. How did it happen? I wasn't hitting on you all along, I wouldn't do that."

"I'm not telling you a thing. If you really don't remember, you can imagine it. Search your memory, maybe it will come back."

She was doing this on purpose, to get me rattled. And she was succeeding. "For all I know, you started it."

"Me!" She shook her head and gave a bitter laugh, as though that was impossible.

I couldn't believe I forced her. Wouldn't. It just wasn't in me. Or was it? I tried to imagine doing that (I couldn't utter the word even to myself) but got nowhere. It wasn't as if she were irresistible. And I don't care for all that wild curly hair she was constantly brushing out of her face. But that was stupid. I knew enough about rape—

not only from Norah but from an old case of Skellings' —to know it was more about power than desire. Why would I want to overpower this harmless girl, at least she was harmless back then. It reminded me of the episodes in Victorian novels I read in college, where the oldest son of the house forces the kitchen maid. And if she gets pregnant she's turned out. Or if the truth comes out, she's set up somewhere in a cottage in the country and the wealthy family supports her, minimally, and the young son gets off with a scolding or maybe is sent off to the army. Years later the child that resulted, now all grown, reappears and threatens to reveal the truth …

My mind was careening, like a wounded bird. We were not living in a Victorian mansion but in our ordinary house, just like the others on the block, where there were no hidden laundry nooks useful for seduction. We didn't have servants who lived in an unheated attic. Where, then? The boys Sandra was taking care of were just three and ten then. It was impossible. Vince was probably old enough to be left alone but not Kevin. (Also old enough to hear any noises or arguments.) It couldn't happen, but evidently it did. DNA doesn't lie. And even if it was simple seduction, it would have been difficult. A quickie with the babysitter in the bathroom? I shuddered. Why wasn't she on the pill? Maybe that was her first time? She was only, what, seventeen back then? This was getting worse the more I thought about it. And worst of all was that I would never know. Unless Sandra had told Norah, who was keeping it to herself. But could Sandra be trusted? She might have made up anything.

Why was it that the few things I had learned about my past were all disgraceful? Susan's story about the accident after the high school prom. She couldn't be lying. Why would she? Anyone could lie to me about anything, and I wouldn't know the difference. Saul's story about how I'd managed to get a major role when it should have gone to someone else? Why wasn't anyone coming forward with stories about my bravery, my honor, my generosity? What if I'd let a fellow student get a leading role because I already had the promise of a small part off Broadway when I'd graduated. Would I do that? Was it in me? Or was I the sort of person who wanted everything for myself?

The terrifying truth was that after over two weeks I still didn't know who or what I was, what I had done, what I was capable of.

Luz had accepted a slice of pizza from Sandra and was munching it. Sitting on my lap had calmed her. I was glad. I didn't want her to be frightened, in case there was ever future contact. Also the rain was coming down harder. Luckily, I'd brought an umbrella, but I'd forgotten Luz's small one decorated with the *Brave* characters she insisted on carrying in the rain. God, I hoped she wouldn't make a fuss about that.

"We have to go now. Come, Luz." I wiped her mouth with a paper napkin from the container on the table. "Thanks for the pizza. Luz, say thank you to Sandra."

"Thank you," she mumbled without looking at Sandra.

"See you tomorrow," Sandra said. "You're very sure of yourself, but you might have a few surprises."

THE NEXT DAY NORAH AND I TOOK LUZ TO preschool, noisy and chaotic with the kids all arriving at once, the wails and shrieks, the backpacks, the miniature umbrellas decorated with cartoon characters, the boots —it was still raining. Yet once outside of that familiar and benign atmosphere I wished the harmless chaos had lasted longer. The noise of four-year-olds was innocent, untroubling. Nowadays, even crowded streets get me anxious, and I was anxious enough about the appointment already. Norah took my arm as she would a blind person's, and soon we were in a taxi headed downtown to the meeting our lawyer had assured us would never take place.

But it was taking place, Howard had explained on the phone the night before, simply to stop Sandra's attorney's persistent calls. He couldn't call it a case—there was no case. But in order to put an end to the whole business, he'd finally agreed to a meeting. "This is highly unorthodox. Most lawyers would hang up on her by this point. But since you're such longstanding clients and to put a stop to any further harassment, I'll arrange something, and that will be the end. She must be pestering her attorney too, she sounds very young, and maybe she doesn't know how to get rid of her."

"Thanks, Howard. I appreciate it."

"It'll cost you, you understand." He cleared his throat. "By the way, that matter you called me about before your accident … Do you still need to discuss it? Not on the phone, of course."

"Let's forget it for now. I'll have to think about that."

Of course it would cost; everything does.

In his office, he stood up to greet us, and I pretended to recognize him as we shook hands. He was gray-haired with a receding hairline, tiny frameless rectangular glasses, and a lawyerly demeanor, that is, as if no dispute were beyond his powers to fix. As if nothing could shake his certainty of who he was, who he had always been. Sandra, who ignored us, was there along with her attorney, a woman in a gray business suit, her hair in a severe bun, who looked barely old enough to have graduated from law school. Rosa, Sandra's aunt, was there as well and shifted uncomfortably in her seat while offering an apologetic shrug. She clearly didn't want Sandra to pursue the "case," but Sandra, as I was discovering, was stubborn.

To my surprise and relief, the meeting was brief, as Howard had predicted.

He began in a frosty tone of utter confidence. "Ms. Gonzalez has explained the wishes of her client. Right before you came in, I was about to inform her and Ms. Morales that they would be unwise to initiate any kind of legal proceedings, which I can tell you right now would go nowhere and simply be a waste of time and money. To put it bluntly, they have no case. Number one, the adoption papers are perfectly in order." He handed a folder to the lawyer. "You can have a look."

"You're aware, of course, that Ms. Morales was under twenty-one when she signed," said the young lawyer.

"Yes, of course, but it was consistent with the law to have her aunt sign as legal guardian."

The young lawyer seemed about to interrupt, but Howard cut her off. "Number two, the cases of surrogate mothers that Ms. Morales referred to when she phoned me have no bearing on this situation, as she well knows. Those cases are entirely different. Besides the issue of surrogate mothers—a very different kettle of fish—those cases deal with infants, while this situation involves a child of almost five years old whom the birth mother has not inquired about since her birth. No judge is going to remove a happy and healthy child from her legal home simply because the birth mother has changed her mind."

"But she's my child," Sandra burst out. "I gave birth to her. Doesn't that matter? I was too young to understand what I was doing."

"Don't you recall that in your allocution almost five years ago you swore under oath that you give up all rights to the child? You signed papers agreeing to the adoption. Changing your mind, for whatever reason, is not legally relevant. Moreover, Mr. Marzino is the biological father of the child; the DNA tests done shortly after the child's birth prove that. That naturally carries a great deal of weight. Number three, not that this issue can be over-turned, mind you, but if circumstances were different, you would have to prove that you can supply a suitable home for the child and be prepared to take on the ex-penses of raising her. From what you've told me, this is not the case. You currently reside in a dormitory in your college."

"We assumed," said the young lawyer, "that Mr. Marzino would be willing and able to help provide for the child."

Howard glanced at Norah and me, but we said nothing, as he had advised us to do. "Say nothing unless it's absolutely necessary, or I address a question to you. Leave the talking to me."

At this point I was wishing I could disappear. That shame and regret could make me invisible.

Howard shifted in his seat, removed his tiny glasses and turned directly to Sandra with a more kindly expres-sion, but righteous, like the lawyers on *Crime City*. "Look, Ms. Morales, I can sympathize with your feelings, anyone can change their mind, but the law is not prepared to deal with fluctuating emotions. If you agree to let the matter drop—as it will be dropped in any event—perhaps Joe and Norah would be willing to come to some arrange-ment about periodic visits."

This suggestion didn't appeal to me at all, seeing that

Sandra's previous attempts to visit Luz—especially the day she grabbed her and raced out of our front door—had resulted only in Luz's terrified tears and our own terror that she was being kidnapped. But again I kept my mouth shut. Norah squeezed my hand as if that could control my tongue.

"I'll have to go over these adoption papers again," said the young lawyer, "and do some more research."

"Of course," said Howard. "Take your time. But I doubt that you'll find anything that would necessitate further meetings. Meanwhile, I think we've done all we can here." He rose and put his glasses back on, making him stern again. We all stood up and started towards the door.

"Don't think you've seen the last of me," Sandra said. "This is far from over. Just because you have the money and a big house doesn't mean you can have my child. Suppose I say you raped me? What would a judge think about that?"

"Sandra," said Howard. "Think. A charge of rape is a very serious thing. You never mentioned that before, and it's unlikely you would be believed after so long. There's no evidence, nothing at all to indicate that. You never went to the police."

Norah's face was furious with rage. She hadn't said a word all along but now she burst out. "Rape! Police! You told me what happened, and it was far from rape! You just couldn't help yourself, you said, you were really … what did you say? Caught up in the moment, didn't realize what you were doing, a momentary thing. When he wanted to stop you … well, you made it hard to stop. When you realized you were pregnant you came to me and cried and begged me to forgive you. I thought you were coming to me for money, but you didn't even have the brains for that. I offered to pay for an abortion, but you and your aunt were against that, and anyhow it was too late. You are a very stupid girl, that's the plain truth, and you should be glad you're free to go to school and know that your child is being raised properly."

"Norah, please, this isn't helping. Why don't you all go home now and calm down." While they were getting their coats on Howard took me aside and whispered, "Don't worry, this will all come to nothing."

"She never told me," I muttered to Howard. "Norah never said anything about Sandra coming to her and crying." I shouldn't have spoken; this was between Norah and me. But I was too stunned for self-control. She'd let me believe she knew nothing about how it happened. She let me think I might have forced the girl, that I was a man who would do that. She allowed me to dread that I might be someone I was not. I should have been relieved, but the relief dimmed under the cloud of my anger. Maybe that was her revenge. Was that enough to warrant divorce? Well, no, not quite enough.

We said nothing in the taxi going home though surely Norah knew what I was thinking. The kids were all still in school. I went up to my small study on the third floor and lay on the couch. I tried to imagine how I would seduce a girl like Sandra. Besides the fact that I couldn't recall seducing anyone. She was too young, too ignorant, too volatile, and all in all too large for my tastes. Maybe she seduced me. But there must have been some event that triggered it. I didn't simply find her and grab her. Or cajole her, why on earth would I? I tried imagining a rape scene, but I couldn't do it. I tried imagining Skellings raping someone he'd interviewed, a witness. I couldn't do that either. Skellings was more likely to control his impulses than I was. But I ended up the father of her child. My dearest Luz. She was not conceived in violence, I was sure of that.

WE WERE LINGERING OVER DINNER AFTER Norah had put Luz to bed and the boys were in their rooms doing whatever they did there, video games, probably. I would deal with that after I had my head together. Norah had seemed distracted all evening. She cooked a delicious lasagna but barely spoke while we were eating it. Maybe she was irked that I hadn't yet taken over my share of the cooking. No, she'd say something about that. She wasn't the sort who let minor grievances fester. Finally, after I lit a cigarette, she spoke.

"Who is Emily?"

"Who is Emily? I don't know. Who is she?"

"She's a woman who called today while you were sleeping to ask how you are and whether you'd be at the studio next week for another photo shoot. You missed one a couple of days ago."

"So she's a photographer?"

"So she says."

"Well, why would she say so if she isn't?"

"I don't know. You tell me."

"What are you getting at?"

"If you were having an affair, you wouldn't even remember, would you? I might even feel sorry for her. If she came looking for you and you didn't recognize her, the way you didn't recognize me at the hospital. Maybe if by some remote chance she'd gotten there first, she would have taken you home with her, and you'd be in another life."

"Norah, this is sounding crazy. It's not like you. My

life is here, we both know that. I don't know any Emily."
I remembered that first day in the hospital, when I had
the same thought myself. Any woman could have walked
in and claimed me. Did they require proof when they
released a patient in someone's care? I didn't recall any
Emily. But then I didn't recall very many people. If we
were having an affair, it was lost in the ether with the rest
of my past. I hoped she wouldn't keep calling.

"Well, if she calls again, I'll put you on, and you can
straighten it out. Maybe her number is in your phone. I
didn't think to look. It's beneath me anyway, to check
your phone."

"I'll look right now." My phone was in my back pocket.
"Here," I handed it to her. "See for yourself, there's no
Emily."

"I'll take your word for it."

"You're making trouble where there is none."

"Let's hope so," she said and began clearing the table.

I GOT HOME FROM REHEARSAL IN MID-
afternoon—in the newest script that we read through
quickly, Skellings tracked down a notorious jewel thief
and rebuffed a seduction by his client, a grateful rich
widow—to find a note from Norah taped to the front
door. I could recognize her handwriting anywhere,
right-leaning, rhythmic and consistent as if done by a
calligrapher. "I'm having a little tea party with Clara Keller,
Kenneth and Frank. A get-to-know-your-neighbors event.
So don't be surprised. The tall thin Black guy is Kenneth,
and the tall thin white one is Frank." She'd mentioned
that she was going to get them together, but I'd thought
she was kidding.

They were in the living room, not at the dining room table as I'd expected, and it wasn't a tea party after all. Ken and Clara's drinks looked like Scotch, more watered down in her glass, and Frank wasn't there at all. Norah must have prepared the note before her guests arrived.

I gave what I hoped was a warm greeting, handshakes all around, to these neighbors I'd apparently known for years, and bent down to kiss Norah, who was drinking red wine. "Join us, sweetheart," in a honeyed voice. "Some wine, or Scotch?"

I opted for the Scotch, figuring I'd need it.

"Frank couldn't make it, sorry to say—an unexpected meeting," Ken announced. "But it's good to see you, Joe, it's been a long time. How's your ankle?"

Norah had made the drink quite strong. "Much better, thanks. Soon I can get rid of the cane." Maybe Ken had thought the tea party would go better with only one of them present. He had some kind of accent, but I couldn't remember where he was from.

"Ken was just telling us about growing up in Martinique," said Norah.

"I don't think I knew that," I said.

"And the interesting thing is that Clara was a French teacher at Bronx Science," she added. "Head of the department."

"Yes," Clara replied eagerly. "I recognized the accent right away. But I couldn't have said Martinique. I thought maybe Paris."

"I did live there for a while when I went to the Sorbonne. That was years ago."

"And now he's teaching," Clara said proudly, as if he'd been her pupil.

"Yes, but only as a stopgap," said Ken. "I'm actually a dancer, and I'm going around auditioning. I'm trying to get into Ailey's company. There might be a male dancer retiring, so that could be my chance."

"A dancer," cried Clara. "How exciting! I love going to dance performances. If you get into the company, will you get me tickets?"

"I'll do my best," he said. "Or if you like, I'll take you one night. I have a friend who works there."

Norah was looking proud and pleased, like a successful matchmaker. I could sense that this was going to turn out well, fortuitously. No comments so far about holding hands on the balcony, or playing with feet. Maybe Clara had assumed that was a Caribbean custom.

"But it might be later in the season. Frank and I are going to Fire Island for a month as soon as school is out."

"Fire Island," Clara said hesitantly. "Isn't that where, uh ..."

"Yes, it's a gay men's haven. We're sharing a house with a couple of other guys."

She took a swallow of Scotch, and I asked, "Where are the kids?" before any further details about Fire Island came up.

"Kevin is at orchestra practice. Vince is upstairs with Samantha. Luz is at a friend's house, and in fact I was going to ask if you might pick her up in a few minutes. Do you have time?"

I leaped at the chance. Little as I knew about myself, I suspected that diplomacy was not one of my strong points. Clara showed no inclination to leave, indeed started a lively conversation with Ken in French as Norah wrote down the address of Luz's friend. I went up to change and was out of there in minutes. Full of admiration for my wife. Perhaps she should have worked in the Foreign Service.

REGARDING HER TALENTS, I WAS STILL preoccupied with what she might be doing to earn extra money, some insignificant part-time work, she said. It wouldn't be something involving a desk and a computer—she had enough of that in her job at the library. She could sing and dance, but if she was auditioning or had gotten a part, I surely would have heard about it; besides, she'd have to quit the library job, and she would have told me. She might be singing in some café, but then she'd be out at night, and she was usually home, unless she was having dinner with a girlfriend. Was she working as a high-class call girl? Daytime work? I thought of Catherine Deneuve in *Belle de Jour*, who was too fastidious to sleep with her husband but spent afternoons in a brothel catering to unusual tastes, which she apparently craved. No, that couldn't be Norah. Or could it? She's not too delicate to sleep with me, but I didn't offer anything especially exotic.

"So now you can tell me," I said to Norah that night, after I congratulated her on her successful diplomacy. Would it be a night of discussing everyone's sexual exploits? "What is this secret job?"

She fiddled around with her hair before answering and gave a slight cough. "I work as a model at the Art Students League. Life studies classes."

I sat up. "You mean you pose naked in front of a whole bunch of people who stare at you and draw you?"

"I guess that pretty much sums it up."

"But why?"

"Well, it brings in some extra money."

"But I thought we didn't need extra money."

"We did when I started. It was a few years ago. Vince needed contact lenses, and Kevin had all that dental work. Luz was starting to walk and getting into everything and had to be constantly watched. It was before *Crime City.* You'd been out of work, and besides, you were just out of the hospital."

"I was in the hospital? What for?"

"Oh, you were having these splitting headaches and finally decided to see a doctor. It turned out you had a sinus infection with an abscess that had to be removed. It was minor surgery, nothing too serious."

"So doctors were fussing inside my head? Why didn't you tell me this before?" I felt the same panic as when I woke in the hospital and couldn't remember anything. What had they done in there? "Maybe it has something to do with my forgetting everything." I was up, striding about the room, terrified that I could never recover my memory, like poor H.M., that they had unwittingly removed some essential pieces of me, irretrievable cells containing my history and tossed out with the hospital trash.

"Oh, calm down. It was painful but not dangerous. But all surgery is dangerous, so we were scared till it was over. It has nothing to do with what's happening now. I told the doctor about it, the one we see now, and he said there was no possible connection."

So my brain had been tampered with, and my wife was posing nude for a bunch of lascivious strangers and getting money for it. Was that any better than being a call girl? "But why that? Couldn't you find any work besides displaying yourself? What's in it for you? I must say I'm surprised. I would never have thought of that. And why didn't you stop when things got better, when I came home and got the job as Skellings?"

"At the time it was the easiest thing I could find. I had so much on my mind, you and the kids and the house, and I could just sit there being still, doing nothing. But, you know … I found I liked it. After things got better at home. I liked being looked at."

"Don't I look at you? Or not enough?"

"It's different. And no, you don't really look at me. You didn't then, and you don't now."

"I don't?"

"No."

"I bet I look as much as other husbands do."

"Since when are other husbands a standard?"

"Norah, let's stop. This is a ridiculous discussion. Okay. So tell me how I should look at you that would turn you on like sitting naked in front of strangers?"

"It doesn't turn me on in the least. I barely see them. I just relax and think. It's at the end of the day, twice a week. I leave work early, I'm tired. I know it sounds silly, but it makes me feel I have some value, I mean besides being a wife and mother and all that. They need models to learn. They look at me intently, and I like it, but it's not about sex. It's more like being onstage, where part of the pleasure is knowing you're being watched closely."

"Really? How do you know what it's about? How do you know they don't go home and jerk off thinking about you? Do you have to spread your legs?" Now I was striding up and back pulling my shirt out of my pants, just to tear at something.

"I knew this would happen if I told you. I'm sorry I did. Because in essence you're a pig, like most men. I should have lied and made up something, maybe like cleaning offices at night. Would that be better? And no, I don't have to spread my legs. Only for you, okay? On demand."

"Oh, come off it. I don't demand, and you like it too. Unless you're pretending."

"Okay, that wasn't fair. But look at the fuss you're making over something harmless that doesn't affect you at all. Except it's a little extra cash."

I sat back down on the bed. Meanwhile she moved around so she was leaning against the pillows and took her book from the bedside table. I couldn't see it, probably some feminist tract listing the sins of men throughout history.

"Do you realize we're having our first real fight since my accident? And while we're at it, why haven't you told me where the car is? You never tell me anything important."

"The car is in a garage on 88th Street. I know it's expensive, but I didn't park on the street because I didn't want to keep moving it every few days. I thought you might need me. Then I just forgot. But otherwise I tell you everything. I've helped you manage since you got home, haven't I? I just shouldn't tell you anything you might not like."

"I don't like this latest, no. But I don't suppose you're going to stop?"

"No, it doesn't do any real harm, and it's relaxing."

"Don't any of them ever ask you out?"

"Yes."

"And what do you say?"

"I say I have to go home and prepare dinner for my husband and children." At this she smiled, and I couldn't help grinning myself.

Then came the *coup de grace*. "And this from a man who got the teenaged babysitter pregnant."

There was nothing I could say to that, so I propped up my pillows and got my book from the bedside table. I was almost finished with the book about Stiller. I'd gotten quite fascinated and kept taking notes. He's back with his wife but doesn't know her secret—that she's quite sick and will soon have to return to the hospital. Sad, but more innocent than my wife's secret.

I HELD MY MOTHER'S ARM AS WE GOT OUT of the elevator. Immediately, the sharp hospital smell hit me, ammonia, cleaning fluid, masking something else—age, decay. The elevator stopped to let people off. Facing us, lined up against the opposite wall, sat men and women in wheelchairs, all in the same hideous white hospital gowns with blue stars, some with their heads slumped on their chests, either sleeping or drugged, some wide-eyed but seeming not to see. A few were mumbling. One woman was calling for a nurse, and a man was weeping silently, wiping his eyes with a paper towel. One called out to us, "Oh, you finally came, now you can get me out of here." I turned to my mother, startled, but she said, "It's always like this, just don't pay attention."

"Is the whole place this way?" I asked. We were at the tenth floor. It was appalling, creepy, to imagine ten floors filled with people in this condition.

"No, no. This is the long-term unit. Usually she's on the hospital floor, but they brought her up here because she has a UTI, I don't know why."

"UTI?"

"Urinary tract infection. It can mess up your mind. They'll give her antibiotics for a few days then send her back down to her room. She has a private room on the eighth floor."

My mother tugged me along. I was afraid she might take my hand, like she was leading a reluctant child.

"It's two doors down," she said. But as we approached

the room, a woman ambling down the hall grabbed my mother's hand. "Wait, I know you," she shouted. "Luisa is your mother-in-law, isn't she? We're friends, you know. My name is Florence."

My mother stopped to talk to her and waved me on. "Go on in, she's in the bed by the window."

Like a child, I was afraid to go in by myself, but I reminded myself I was not a child even though I was on an outing with my mother to visit a sick relative. It was my grandmother we'd come to see, the grandmother who was 93 years old and kept asking about me. The grandmother who'd told me stories and taught me songs. Like a child, I petulantly wished I could have just one song, one story. I hadn't wanted to come but had no good excuse; no rehearsals today and I had plenty of time. What I'd done with this time before the accident, I didn't know. Running, playing squash with Saul?

A white curtain was around the first bed, on the left; I moved on to my grandmother's side of the room, which had a fine view of the Hudson River and the Palisades. I would have liked to gaze for a while but forced myself to regard the woman in the bed. She was lying on her back, asleep and snoring slightly. Her white hair was sparse and straggly, her face wrinkled. A face I had loved. I didn't even feel nostalgia. Her hospital gown had risen up to her stomach and the covering sheet was down at her ankles, exposing her sex, almost hairless but for a few gray strands. The slit and labia looked like a child's. I had just given Luz a bath the night before, and it looked the same, only not as plump and rosy. I stared. Of course I should cover her up, but I was afraid that would wake her and she'd be mortified to have been discovered that way. This only lasted a few seconds. Before I could do anything my mother was in the room, grabbing the sheet and raising it to cover her.

"What are you staring at?" she said angrily. "Haven't you ever seen a woman before? Why didn't you cover her up?"

"I didn't want to wake her." The words sounded pathetic.

"Oh, grow up." My mother rearranged the gown and sheet, and then shook her mother-in-law's shoulder gently. "Luisa, Luisa, I'm here with Joe. Remember you asked about him? Wake up."

The figure in the bed stirred and opened her eyes. They were pale blue in a web of wrinkles. She stared at us blankly for a moment, then said, "Dorrie, is that you? Who's that with you?"

"It's Joe, Luisa. Your grandson. Freddy's boy." She nudged me, again as if I were a child, until I finally greeted my grandmother and bent down to kiss the mottled cheek.

"How are you feeling, Grandma?"

"Nonna. You always called her Nonna, you know, in Italian. That's what she liked."

"Nonna," I said.

"I don't know," the cracked voice came. "I don't know why I'm here." She gazed around. "This isn't my room."

"That's right, Luisa. You have a slight infection, and you'll be here just a few days until it's gone. Then you'll be back in your own room. Do you feel okay? Did you have a good lunch?"

"I don't remember. Who is Joe again?"

"Your grandson." My mother was very patient with her, very kind. Had she been that kind and patient with us? Somehow I doubted it. "Don't you remember Joe and Susan, the twins?"

"Did I have twins?" the old woman asked.

"No, not yours. The twins are mine."

"You're Dorothy. Freddy's wife."

"Right! That's very good. I was here just a few days ago."

"But who's the other one? I had more sons."

"That's Willy. He's your other son."

"I'm having trouble remembering him. Where is he now?"

"Willy is in the Army. A captain."

"That's nice. I hope he isn't in any danger."

"No, he's stationed in Texas."

I didn't remember any Willy either. The farce of it all made me want to laugh aloud, and I was almost afraid I would. Two people with no memories trying to reconstruct a past. Two people who had loved each other.

We didn't stay long because Nonna fell asleep. "What about this Willy?" I asked my mother. "I didn't even know about him."

She gave a sour laugh. "You're as bad as she is. He's your dad's younger brother. He was a favorite of yours when you were a kid. He took you for horsie rides on his shoulders. Oh, and he was the one who taught you to drive."

At the mention of driving I wanted to leave the subject immediately. But my mother wasn't finished. "And I don't suppose you remember Barry?"

"I know he died in the 9/11 attack."

"So you know all about that?"

"Not all. I don't remember the day, I mean my day, but I know what happened. They showed it enough times on TV."

"Barry was the only one of them who made any real money. He was always the smart one. He became a banker.

And look where it got him."

To my surprise, my mother suddenly sank into a chair in the lobby and began to cry.

I sat down and put my arm around her. "I'm so sorry. Susan and I talked about him the other day. How awful. Did he have a family?"

"Yes, a wife and kids, but they were on the verge of divorce. Isn't that ironic? The disaster meant she didn't have to go through the hassle of a divorce. Don't they say every cloud has a silver lining?" She sobbed and bent her head to her chest. "He worked in the first building, on one of the highest floors. He was one of those people who jumped. Do you remember those photos of people jumping out the window, holding hands?"

I didn't, but I nodded.

"You called me to come and stay with Vince, and I did. We were still living in the city at the time. It was before your father …"

"Before he …? Died?"

"Before we found him in a filthy lot somewhere in the Bronx. Susan and I were in a total state of shock. You took over and handled everything. You didn't want the police involved, you headed them off and said it must have been a robbery because he was in the habit of carrying large sums of money around. Which was true. He had dealings with a casino in Connecticut and often carried piles of cash. I don't know why, and I don't want to know. They have safes in those places, but he said it was safer with him, he'd deposit it in the morning."

"So many tragedies," I said. Just for something to say. I could barely believe I had lived through all this and forgotten it. Too much to forget. Or else too much to remember.

"No more than any other family," she said, "except

for Barry. That didn't have to be. There were people who didn't go into work that day, for one reason or other. And there were people who didn't belong there at all. Just chance. Tourists. Delivery people. You know. I thought the hospitals would be crowded. Everyone did. But they weren't. People were either safe or dead. Enough of this," she said finally. "Let's go."

"Do you want to get some lunch first?" I asked.

"No, I just want to go home."

THAT NIGHT MY MOTHER'S FACE AS SHE WEPT kept coming back to me. I imagined myself at her age, in my sixties, say, still without a memory. But with many years behind me, the years starting from now: I could remember those. The kids were grown and had children of their own. The idea made me dizzy, and I couldn't sleep, so I went downstairs to lie on the couch and luckily found some dull movie to watch. Then on my way back up, I heard light footsteps in the hall. Vince's room was on the second floor, opposite ours. When I reached the top of the stairs, I saw a young girl coming out of the bathroom, long blonde hair, in a floaty short white nightie. This was hardly an apparition to frighten me, but what—who—was it? She looked like a forest sprite.

"Well, hello. Can you tell me who you are and what you're doing here?"

"Hi, Mr. Marzino. I'm Samantha. I guess you don't remember me. I was here a few times before with Vince."

"Samantha. Of course. So what are you doing here in the middle of the night?"

"Well," and here she began to look uncomfortable, twirling the ribbons on her white nightie. "A bunch of us went to a basketball game and then we went for pizza, and by that time it was so late I didn't want to take the subway alone—I live in the Village—so Vince said I could stay here. I didn't think I'd disturb anyone, and I'd leave early in the morning."

Vince with a girl. In his narrow single bed. He was going to be sixteen in a couple of weeks. Maybe I shouldn't be surprised. And I already knew her, it seemed.

"Do your parents know you're here?"

"Oh, yes, I called them."

"Okay, well, go back to bed, and I guess I'll see you in the morning."

She walked quickly to Vince's door, the nightie swirling around her thighs. She had nothing on underneath and tried to tug it down. "I'm sorry I disturbed you."

"Not a problem." Of course it was a problem; we'd have to talk to Vince about this, but not at two-thirty in the morning. For all I knew she'd stayed here before, maybe was a regular visitor—and Norah had forgotten to tell me, with all the other things she'd neglected to tell me.

I couldn't get that short nightie out of my mind. I wanted to wake Norah and climb on top of her, but she was sleeping soundly, so I let her be. I took care of my stiff dick as quietly as I could and fell asleep fast.

IT WAS STILL DARK WHEN I WAS AWAKENED by music. Something lively that the musician was having difficulty with, stopping and repeating short passages. Even though I was groggy from sleep, and a bizarre dream about my parents that I couldn't remember, I recognized Kevin's clarinet coming from downstairs. He was anxious about the upcoming auditions—needlessly, for very few of the kids at school studied the clarinet, and Kevin was the best of them, as he'd reminded me. We'd told him, if he was compelled to practice at night, he should do it downstairs in the kitchen. He must have forgotten to close the door. I tried to identify the music. It sounded like Bach or Vivaldi, something sprightly like that. After a few minutes that stopped, and he started the tune of some popular TV show, not *Crime City*, some kids' show I'd overheard. He was gifted, and he could play by ear.

I was mesmerized by the sounds traveling up the stairs. They were trying to awaken something in my brain, the way a dream drifts away so fast but sometimes leaves a clue, a sound or image, or something even more evanescent, and if you don't try too hard and let it alone, it might bring the dream back. There was a peculiar quality of distance, the sound muffled because our bedroom door was closed.

What I heard when Kevin paused for a moment wasn't real music but the sound of knocking, someone rapping on a wall. I lay still and tried not to struggle for the memory, and then I had it. It was the rhythm Susan and I used to rap on the wall together after we went to bed. We'd slept in the same room till we were about ten or so, and then our parents put us in separate but adjacent rooms. We missed being together, and we developed a system of rapping rhythms on the wall— one of us would start, and the other would take it up, and we'd go back and forth until we got sleepy. Sometimes it was the theme song from *Sesame Street* or *The Electric Company*, sometimes the familiar Dah, dah dah dum dum, Dah Dum! Or sometimes one of us would make something up and test the other until we both had it. It was our way of staying together in our separate rooms. We even had a special signal for Good night, I'm tired. It was the rhythm for Night night, sleep tight, don't let the bedbugs bite.

I was so excited—stunned, really—at the return of this memory that I wanted to call Susan right away at her hotel and talk about it. Maybe it was a sign of my past returning. I couldn't remember anything else though. No, I did remember the color of the wall, a pale yellow, and my bed right against the wall as her bed was too. I had some cartoon character on my sheet and pillow, and the quilt too had a super hero—I could see it now, maybe Captain Marvel. I could remember the soft feel of the bed and the pleasure of rapping out Good Night and curling under the covers. I had a piece of my life back and was so astonished I thought I would weep. Next to me, Norah lay sleeping soundly; I didn't want to wake her and tell her. It was my secret, mine and Susan's, as it had been all through our childhood.

I didn't care how late it was. I had to call her. Not downstairs though, where Kevin was practicing. I tiptoed to the study upstairs carrying my phone. She answered sleepily but sounded alarmed.

"What is it, Joe? Are you okay?"

"Yes, fine, don't worry. But I need to talk to you."

"What could possess you to call me at this hour? I thought maybe there was a fire or something."

I told her how I'd heard the notes of Kevin's clarinet drifting up the stairs and through the bedroom door. And then I held the phone near the desk where I was sitting and rapped the rhythm to *The Electric Company*.

"Do you know what that is?"

She was silent. I thought she might rap back, but

she didn't.

"But you must remember, Susan, don't you?"

"Of course I remember. How could I forget?"

"Do you realize, this is the first real memory to come back to me! Maybe it means it will all come back soon." In a confusing flurry, I wondered, like a hailstorm? Or bit by bit? Snatches of brain cells rearranging themselves in my head as I went through the days all unawares?

"Hey Joe, that's great. I'm happy for you. Who knows what might come next? There might be things you don't want to remember."

"No, no, everything I remember is good, even if it's bad. Susan! I'm going to get my life back."

She was silent for a moment. "You're not sleeping again, are you?" I asked. "I'm sorry to call so late, but I had to …"

"No, I'm not sleeping."

"So what is it. Why aren't you excited for me?"

"Do you remember when we stopped?"

"No, when?"

"It was the night of the accident. When you all arranged that I would take the blame. That was when it stopped. We stopped tapping out Good night. And everything else."

I couldn't speak. I had no memory of it stopping.

"We got to our rooms finally after that dreadful night, and a few minutes later, about as long as it would take you to get undressed, you knocked on the wall. But I didn't knock back. I didn't knock back ever again."

"Did I keep knocking?"

"For a few nights. Then you stopped too."

I could hear her crying quietly. "Susan, please. I'm so sorry. I wish I could undo it."

"It didn't seem so to you then. You hardly thought

about it. At least you didn't talk about it." She cried some more, then quieted and said, "Look Joe, I understand this is important. Let's meet tomorrow, I'll help you, and maybe you'll remember some more. But good night for now." And she hung up.

I fell asleep with my head on the desk and the phone in my hand.

I MUST HAVE GOTTEN MYSELF BACK TO BED. Early the next morning I went downstairs and found Luz alone in the kitchen in her Wonder Woman pajamas, pouring Cheerios into a bowl.

"Hi sweetie, you're up early." I kissed the top of her head.

"Mommy lets me make my own breakfast sometimes. Today is Sunday, you know. No school."

"I know."

"But could you pour the milk? I sometimes spill it."

I poured the milk and was starting to make a pot of coffee when she said, "I saw the Tooth Fairy."

"Did I hear you right? The Tooth Fairy? Who lost a tooth? Kevin has his teeth, and you're too young."

"But I saw her. She had long blonde hair and a white lacy dress and bare feet. I couldn't see her wings, but they were probably folded up."

"The Tooth Fairy. Uh-huh. Where did you see her?"

"In the hall. She was going towards Vince's room." Luz giggled. "That was silly because Vince has all his teeth already."

"He certainly does. Did you talk to her?"

"Oh, no. You're not supposed to see the Tooth Fairy. She wouldn't like it if anyone saw her. So I just peeked and went into the bathroom."

"She must have made a mistake and come to the wrong house," I commented.

"Yes, because next door Luke just lost a tooth. I saw him yesterday, and he showed me. It was so loose, it was wobbling around, but he was afraid to pull it out."

"That must be it. Well, I hope she realized her mistake and went next door."

"Daddy?"

"Yes?" The coffee was done, and I poured myself a cup.

"Could you make me a scrambled egg? I'm not allowed to turn on the stove."

"Sure, sweetheart." I took two eggs from the fridge and cracked them into a bowl, as I must have done dozens of times. I knew exactly what to do, and I was grateful.

"Daddy, did the Tooth Fairy come when you were a boy?"

"Of course. Why wouldn't she? It wasn't that long ago. She came for me and for Aunt Susan."

"Did she come for Monica too?"

"No, Monica didn't live with us. She met Susan after they were grown up. Now it's like … they're married. But back then it was just Susan and me. We were twins, you know."

"I know, but you don't look alike."

"Boy twins and girl twins usually look alike, but boys and girls not so much."

"I wish I had a twin."

"Why?"

"Then I'd always have someone to play with. And someone who looked like me, you know, dark with smooth hair." She held out her arm and put it next to mine. "You see?" She chattered on about dark-skinned boy twins in her preschool group while I drifted off. Susan and I had the same skin color, but we differed in so many ways. Susan had believed in the Tooth Fairy. I told her it was nonsense, that fairies couldn't fly into people's houses and search under their pillows, but she persisted in believing. Whenever I found a silver dollar under my pillow, she said, "You see, I told you. She comes even if you don't believe in her." I could have reminded her about the bowl of coins on the lowest kitchen shelf, where my mother kept change for the washing machine and dryer in the basement—this was early on, when we still lived in a Bronx apartment house, before we moved to Dobbs Ferry.

We must have been about ten when we moved. We had stopped arguing about the Tooth Fairy, and I never even tried to enlighten her about Santa Claus. My mother had been angry enough over the Tooth Fairy. "Why don't you let her keep her illusions?" she scolded. "Because it's not real," I said, "and besides it's so silly." I could see this same attachment to facts in Kevin—he often corrected us about small things that didn't matter. But I didn't meddle in Christmas. On Christmas mornings when we came into the living room to find the presents under the tree, I even managed to say, "Look what Santa brought me," about a set of Lincoln logs, and my mother looked at me with relief.

"Daddy, Daddy, I dropped my toast."

"Well, pick it up." My voice sounded so harsh. Not like me at all. I said more gently, "I mean, you're a big girl now, Luz. I bet you can even put a new slice in the toaster, can't you, sweetheart? Then I'll butter it for you."

Mommy, I dropped my napkin. That was my voice. "Well, pick it up, I'm not your servant." And that was my mother's. I heard her as if she were in the room with us. She was upset about something, she wasn't usually harsh, but I didn't know what.

The move was a major project, and my mother kept assuring us we would like the new house. My parents had spent days packing up—my mother wrapped all the china and glassware in newspaper, and I admired how adept she was at rolling the paper around the glasses and tucking it in at the top. She gave us cartons for our toys and games, and we worked industriously to get everything to fit. Then four big men arrived with dollies and loaded all our boxes in their trucks, and finally the furniture. Last thing was to roll up the rugs. Without them, the bare floors were a lighter color than the wood around them, and the apartment looked eerie; I wanted to get going as soon as we could. My father drove, and we sang songs in the car. The bear went over the mountain, because we passed through low mountains, and when we finally arrived, we found the moving truck had gotten there first. The men were standing around outside smoking and waiting for us. It took much less time to unload everything than it had to pack and get it on the truck. They let me help, or pretend to help, with some of the smaller items. In what seemed like just a few minutes the truck was emptied, and our new house, a gray ranch style on a two-acre lot, was filled. My mother stood with her hands on her hips and said, "How will I ever get all of this unpacked and put away?" My father sat on the couch in the living room—that was the first thing they unpacked—and smoked a cigar that smelled terrible, and my mother went around opening all the windows.

She sat down next to him even though she hated the smell of the cigar smoke, and stretched out her legs. She was wearing jeans and blue sneakers. She sent us outside to play, but having grown up on the city streets, we didn't know what to do with the stretch of lawn. We were used to playing in the streets and in the playground three blocks away; the last few months, she'd started letting us walk there by ourselves. This was before everyone had cell phones so we had to promise to be home at a certain time. We each had Mickey Mouse watches.

Susan and I stood on the lawn and looked around. "Do you like it?" I asked, and she shook her head and said, "I don't know yet. Do you?" I said I didn't. I missed my friends from the street. We began throwing a ball around without much enthusiasm. A boy from across the street came over wheeling his bicycle and talked to us. That felt better. He was about our age and was curious about our being twins. His name was Bobby. Bobby Frankel. We had to explain that we were fraternal twins, not identical. He said he had two older brothers and a baby sister. He wanted to see our house, but I explained it was full of cartons and furniture, there wasn't even enough room to walk around. Soon two girls and a boy from nearby houses joined us, and Susan and I felt better.

All of this played like a movie in my head as I sat at the kitchen table watching Luz eat her scrambled eggs. She ate so slowly, and played with the bits of egg on the plate, like she was building a mound. I was mesmerized by what she was doing, and at first I didn't grasp that I was remembering—they were simply scenes played out on the stage of my mind. But when the name Bobby Frankel came to me, I realized these were memories. Not fantasies or recalling some scene I'd played on a stage. It had all happened. I was stunned and wanted to run upstairs and tell Norah, but she wouldn't remember any of it. It wasn't her life. It was Susan I needed.

Then Norah appeared, dressed in a Chinese silk robe

that I recognized as my last year's birthday present. It was shades of orange and gold and brown, and I remembered thinking in the store how well it would go with her hair. She came over and put her arm around me, then gave Luz a kiss on the cheek. "I see you've already had breakfast."

"Daddy made me breakfast. Oh, and I saw the Tooth Fairy last night."

"You did?" Norah rubbed her eyes and blinked.

"Yes, she had her wings and her fairy gown and everything."

"That's nice, dear. Is there any coffee?" she asked me.

"This is still hot." I got up. "You know, Susan believed in the Tooth Fairy also."

"Doesn't everyone?"

"Did you know my family used to live in the Bronx, but we moved to Dobbs Ferry when Susan and I were about ten?"

"Yes, I knew. So what?" She paused and stared at me. "Did you just remember that?"

"Yes, and a lot else too. I have to talk to her."

"How did this happen?"

"I don't know. It just happened. I said something to Luz, and it sounded like my mother's voice. I'm going over to her hotel and see her. I may be a while. I called her during the night when I remembered something."

"Wait, this is important." Suddenly she was wide awake. "What was it you remembered?"

"Oh, just something we used to do as kids. Nothing important."

"It's all important, Joe."

"I know, I know. I'll tell you later. Now I'll call her and get dressed. Here's the coffee."

"It's going to rain again. Take an umbrella."

"Now you sound like my mother. There's a memory."

AN HOUR OR SO LATER SUSAN AND I WERE sitting outside a diner on Broadway, eating cheeseburgers. It hadn't rained after all. It turned sunny and warm, almost May weather, and a big umbrella shielded us.

"Later today I've got to bring some of Monica's work to the Cooper Hewitt Museum—they're planning a show of contemporary pottery. Maybe you can help me."

"Sure, I'll drive you over." Then I remembered the car was still in the garage. "Or probably a cab would be better. Say around three? By the way, does Monica know about our past, the move, Dad's death and all?"

"No. I never talk about any of that. Colorado is far away, and it's easy to put things behind me. She's different, she likes to talk about her past. In Jamaica her parents had a restaurant, so she's a great cook. Anyhow, even if I don't talk about it, I don't forget, like you do."

"No, I'm the forgetter."

"You must have more to forget." She waved to the waiter for another coffee, which she drank black while it was still steaming, as I did.

I told her what I remembered about our move to Dobbs Ferry, and she confirmed all my memories. I was hoping they weren't some fantasy my mind cooked up, just to feel I was getting better. She even remembered the names of the moving men, Steve and Artie, who let her help them wheel the dollies. And Bobby Frankel, the boy from across the street, who she said she later necked with in the dark on our back patio. "That wasn't worth remembering," she said with a laugh. "But the most dramatic thing about the move was the next day. We were settled in our rooms and slept on mattresses because the beds weren't set up yet."

"Yes, I remember that! We still shared a room then."

"Yes, we were ten. But I mean what we did early that morning?"

"What?"

"We wanted to explore the house while Mom and Pop were still sleeping. So we couldn't run around making noise. We looked in our closet and there was a metal ladder against a back wall—we could see it because there weren't any clothes hung up yet. So we decided to climb up and see what was there."

I listened, mystified; as far as I knew, this had never happened to me.

"I went first," she continued. "At the top was a square door with a kind of pole hanging on the wall. I didn't know what to do, but you, you were right behind me, and you figured out how to put the pole in a groove in the door and shove it open and fix it in place. So once we got it positioned, we just ... went out, I went first, and there we were on the roof."

"A flat roof?"

"Yes, tar, and luckily it wasn't very hot that day. It was summer, remember, they arranged the move so we wouldn't miss any school."

"I remember the last day of school but none of this about the roof. So what could we see?"

"Well, it felt very exciting, but it was only all the other almost identical suburban houses in the development, with their lawns and driveways and all the rest. God, how I came to hate that neighborhood. Anyway, that first day it was a thrill; we could see the highway a ways off and a bit of a shopping center with its big signs, Macy's, McDonalds, Gino's Pizzeria ... There was no one out, it probably wasn't even seven in the morning. We walked around the roof, feeling like we'd discovered a new continent. We made plans for the things we would do up there. We could have a club and have the neighborhood kids come, the ones who came over to our lawn the day before. We could set up games, darts, archery. I already loved horses and thought maybe we could get a horse and put a stable on the lawn below. It was big enough."

"Why don't I remember any of this?"

"Well, how would I know, Joe? Maybe the memories come back in pieces. You should ask your doctor. You do have someone you see about this, don't you?"

"Sure." That bald guy Norah and I had seen a week ago who had tried to assure us my memory would return, but he hadn't sounded optimistic. Now I was looking forward to telling him, to prove him wrong. If not for that clarinet music in the middle of the night, Kevin practicing for the band auditions, maybe I wouldn't have remembered the rapping on the wall, and all the rest that came tumbling after, an avalanche in my head …

"And if you're the same as I remember," said Susan, "you probably scoured the internet for whatever you could find out about memory loss."

"You're right," I said, and ate the last of the cheeseburger, which had been remarkably good. I hadn't had a cheeseburger since before the accident, and I remembered now how I loved them. That and quesadillas, which I used to get at a little Mexican place on Amsterdam Avenue. Suddenly it seemed there was a banquet awaiting in my memory, all the foods I'd loved to eat—how could I have forgotten them? It seemed almost as disloyal as forgetting my family.

"Not only that, but I watched lots of movies where guys lose their memories. Somehow it's always men, at least the ones I saw. It's a movie cliché, and according to the doctor, not usually accurate. Did you ever see *Random Harvest*?"

She sneered. "Ronald Colman. God, that was the pits. Reach for your hankies, folks."

"I loved it."

"You were always a sucker for sentiment. A softie. Like that detective on your show. Everyone can tell that beneath that tough exterior he has a heart of gold."

"But I don't have a tough exterior."

"No, you don't. So anyway there we were up on the roof checking out the neighborhood. It wasn't very high—it was a low ranch house. We probably could have jumped down, and later on we did. But we didn't want to wake them up, this was too much fun."

"I've forgotten the best things."

"But you must remember, after a while, hearing Mom screaming downstairs?"

"No."

"She got up and couldn't find us anywhere. She woke Pop up, and they went through the whole house. She was hysterical. So I decided we'd better get down. Which was not as easy as getting up. We had a hard time getting that door back in place, and they must have heard. We rushed down the ladder and saw her in our room yelling like a wild woman. She must have thought we ran away or were kidnapped or something. It took a while for her to calm down, after she finished screaming with relief."

"Why the hysteria? We must have been somewhere."

"Because of Tommy. She was yelling, I already lost one, please God don't take the others away from me."

"Who's Tommy?"

Susan set down her cup carefully as if she were afraid it might break, and stared at me. "Don't tell me you don't remember Tommy? That's really ... too scary, Joe."

"I don't. Tell me."

"He was our brother. He was just a couple of years

younger, and when he was still a toddler … he got sick and died. Joe, are you with me?"

I must have stared for a long time. Stunned by what I could forget. Of all that I'd forgotten, this must be the worst. "You're not kidding me, are you?"

"Joe, would I joke about something like this? It was awful. He was just a toddler running around, and we played with him, and then one day he got sick. That's how it seemed. One day he was fine, and the next day he was in bed barely conscious, and we weren't allowed to go into the room, he had a little room just opposite ours, but they wouldn't let us see him. We cried, both of us. We knew something terrible was going to happen, we even talked about whether he could die, we hardly knew what dying was, but we understood this must be it, from the way Mom and Pop acted, and the doctors. They didn't even take him to the hospital. The doctors said they couldn't do anything more for him there, so Mom and Pop said he should stay home."

"But what was it?"

"Meningitis."

There were tears in her eyes, and I was tearing up too. Not just for the loss, so sudden and startling now, but for my forgetting. This was worse than fucking the babysitter, worse than blaming the auto accident on Susan. And worse was my making a hierarchy of my bad deeds; possibly these were only the beginning. Worst of all was that I hadn't forgotten Tommy after my accident with the cyclist. No, I must have forgotten him years ago, when I was a small child and couldn't allow such grief to lodge in my mind. So I erased it just as efficiently as I used to shake my Etch A Sketch drawings from the magic pad.

"I don't … I don't think I can accept that. That I

forgot. What does that make me?"

"It didn't help that Mom didn't let us talk about him. We were only four, remember, and she must have thought that, if he was never mentioned, we would forget, and we would be happier that way."

"Could she really believe that?"

"Well, maybe not, but remember she was so devastated. And she got Pop not to talk about him, either. He may have been tough in the world outside, but at home she was boss. His face changed, he got older, he stopped shaving for a while and looked awful. They got rid of all the baby furniture and toys and all. They made it seem as if he had never been. If I lost a child, I think I would have done the opposite. Saved everything and kind of made a little altar. What about you?"

"I can't even contemplate it."

We sat silently for a long time, sipping at the tepid coffee. "So that was how I handled things, right? Forgetting?"

"Just Tommy, as far as I know. I used to try to remind you, but you didn't want to listen, and you'd start doing something else, like banging on your toy drum, something that made noise, to shut out my words. But you didn't forget what you did the night of the accident. You couldn't look me in the eye for a while."

"There are so many kinds of forgetting. I'd never have remembered Tommy if you hadn't told me. I'm so ashamed."

"That's the most intimate thing you've said to me since we got here."

"That makes it worse. What about when Pop died? Did she hush that up too?"

"I don't know any more about that than you do, or did. He was found in an empty lot in the Bronx. He'd been shot, but somehow it never made the papers, it was handled very quietly. His friends took care of that, and then you helped with all the arrangements."

"That's what Norah told me. It must have been the Skellings in me. I'm surprised we didn't try to investigate more." Yes, Skellings would have been good at that. He'd have known how to deal with those characters.

"She wouldn't allow it, Mom, I mean. We were all grown up, and we couldn't do a thing. Practically five minutes later she moved somewhere else in Westchester and started a new life. She became a new person."

"I must have noticed, didn't I?"

"Sure you did, but she's so stubborn. Just like with Tommy, she wouldn't talk about it anymore. She did the things a widow is supposed to do, grieved for a while, and then, it was like she took on a new identity. You know, the job, the clothes and what not."

"Yes, I've seen her. You haven't seen her yet, have you?"

She shook her head.

"We'll have you over for dinner with her. Tomorrow."

"That'll be easier without Monica. She thinks Monica made me gay, which is ridiculous. I knew when I was back in high school. Monica is bisexual. Every now and then she sneaks off to have a fling with some guy. It doesn't really bother me, that's how she is. As long as she's careful."

WE WENT TO BED LATE THAT NIGHT AFTER a talk with Vince. Of course they were sleeping together, was I living in the Dark Ages?—everyone in school did. Well, almost everyone except for a few weird kids. Yes, he used protection, and moreover, she was on the pill. The most we could accomplish was that he would ask our permission when she slept over. He couldn't sleep at her house—her father wouldn't allow it. A stronger father than I was, clearly. Norah and I didn't stay up to talk about it. "I've had a long day," she said, turned out the light, and rolled over.

Monday I woke up restless. I decided to get in touch with my friend Saul, who'd given me the novel that got me so angry. But I wanted to talk to him when no one was around. Family life was full of interruptions, comings and goings, and I'd be trying to study the next script, the one about a killer of old women, like Raskolnikov. I thought again briefly of the Tooth Fairy. Let the fairy's mother tell her a few things. I was tired of the present. The past, which was returning to me in disorganized patches, was easier to deal with despite its miseries. It was over. So much easier than a life in progress.

So I emailed Saul, in a more civil tone than I'd used on the phone, and asked if he stayed up late—something I should have known if we were such good friends—and if I might call him around midnight or one. There was something I wanted to talk about. As soon as I sent it, I recalled vaguely that he lived in the neighborhood—I might have suggested we meet in a bar or coffee house.

Sure, he said. He was a night owl. Why didn't I come by and ring his bell, it was only half a mile away, near the other park, Riverside. We could sit on a bench on the Drive and have a couple of beers. "We've done that before, remember? Or maybe you don't." As soon as he said it, I did remember.

I found him gazing out at the river, which was barely visible with the trees so dense with leaves. To our left was a cluster of pink and white magnolia trees, just starting to flower, lit up by the streetlamps, like an eerie stage set. I remembered how I used to come down here every early spring with Luz and Kevin to show them the trees in full bloom—they were so splendid and lasted only a few days. If you put it off, you could miss them.

"I wanted to talk about that book again. Stiller?"

"Oh, did you finish it? I had the impression you didn't like it."

"No, I wouldn't say that. It was quite good, as a matter of fact. Could make a good play. What ticked me off was that you should suggest I was like that guy, pretending. He knew all along who he was, he just didn't want that identity anymore. Simply refused it." I took out the notepad where I'd jotted down sentences as I read. "But of course by the end he accepts it. He has no choice. He says … 'I threw away a life that had never been a life.'"

"But that doesn't apply to you. You had a real life. You still do."

"Yes, but it turns out not to have been the life I would have imagined I had, or I would have liked to have had, if that makes any sense."

"I shouldn't have tried to play amateur psychologist. Sorry if you got that impression. It was just so bizarre to see you denying the obvious. I mean, like everyone in the neighborhood knows you're Skellings and thinks it's funny because you're so unlike him in life. You know, you help old ladies cross the street, help at the recycling, stuff like that."

We both laughed. "Actually Skellings would help old ladies too. He's not such a bad guy. Anyhow, it happens that I've got some of my memory back, just small bits—"

"Hey, good news, man!"

"But it's not all good news. Some of it I can't even talk about. Like, I did something awful to Susan when we were teenagers—I shudder every time I think of it, I'm so ashamed, frankly."

"You don't mean …"

"No, no, nothing sexual. Just a … bad betrayal. And just the other day she told me more about my father's death. It was hushed up, but it sounds like he was killed. Low-level gangster stuff."

"And you never knew?"

"I don't remember how much I knew. It wasn't that long ago, about ten years. I made all the funeral arrangements, they tell me. I was a good son."

"You never told me much about it."

"No, we weren't supposed to talk about it." I was surprised to find myself confiding these things to Saul, but as I spoke I remembered what close friends we'd been. We told each other things that men don't usually reveal. He had told me about his divorce, how he had hit his wife and knocked her to the floor and she got a restraining order. He'd cried when he told me. "I'm not that kind of guy," he kept repeating. "I'm just not that kind of guy, how could I do that?" I could sympathize with that. I didn't feel like the kind of guy I was turning out to be. Our closeness hadn't been real for me that day he came to the house with the book, just because he didn't fit my image of a friend. Now all the details were back, and the feelings along with them.

"The way I feel now, or the way I felt before the memories started returning, is like what Stiller says after he admits he's Stiller. Listen to this. 'The present suffices me to an extent that is often astounding.'"

"Doesn't sound too bad," said Saul, lighting a cigarette and offering one to me.

"No, it could be worse, and yet it kind of closes things off. I didn't know till just the other day that I had a baby brother who died at about two. Susan told me. She and I were four. Meningitis. I don't remember the sickness, just a lot of people coming to the house and lots of food around. That must have been after the funeral. Susan and I didn't go, a neighbor took care of us. After, my mother would never talk about it, we weren't supposed to mention his name, and she cleaned out his room as if he'd never been. And I guess I forgot. I don't mean forgot now, I mean forgot back then, as I grew up. He was with us for such a short time. I don't know how I could forget, but maybe I'm like that Stiller, I just pretend to myself that things never happened, and after a while they do disappear. Susan remembered, though. The only reason I remember now is that she reminded me the other day. She couldn't understand how I could put him out of my mind so easily. Well, maybe it wasn't easily, but I must have done my best to forget."

"That's a sad story," said Saul. "I'm sorry."

"So with all this wretched stuff I forgot, I got to thinking maybe I wasn't so far from Stiller. I mean, he remembers—that he treated his wife badly, that he was a lousy sculptor, or so he thinks, that he purposely lost touch with his family, his brother … Maybe I was forgetting on purpose."

"But this time you were really hit on the head. They found brain injuries, didn't they?"

"Yes. But now that stuff is coming back, which is what ordinarily happens, at least that's what the doctor expected, why isn't the bad stuff coming back? Susan had to tell me those awful things. There are still a couple of things I can't get back that would make a big difference …"

We sat there in the dark for a long time. A bunch of teenage boys came zooming by on bikes, slowed down

and looked us over, then went on. We barely noticed—
we were both so used to the neighborhood and rarely
felt threatened by its late-night capers. We opened two
more beers from the six-pack, and we smoked. Watched
a barge slide past slowly. A couple came by walking a
crying baby in a carriage; it brought back memories of
sleepless nights with our babies. Luz was the calmest,
I remembered, an easy baby. Vince was the worst, but
maybe that was because he was the first and we had no
experience. After a while it started to drizzle, and we
headed for home. We passed Saul's house first, and I
continued on my own.

THE NEXT GRAY AFTERNOON—IT SEEMED
to rain so often; was it like this every spring?—I was
going over the next script for *Crime City*. Everyone was
out, and I was relaxing with my feet up on the couch.
I was eager to see what Skellings, whom I'd come to
think of as my alter ego or my better half, rather than
my evil twin, was up to now. Imagine my surprise when
the script began not with a desperate client seeking help,
but with a scene between Skellings and his often-neglected
girlfriend, Cheryl, in Cheryl's living room. They were
sitting on a couch side by side with the Sunday papers
spread out between them when Cheryl opened with,
"There's something I've got to tell you, Ralph." He puts the
paper aside, *"reluctantly,"* it read, and turns to her. I imagined him lighting a cigarette at this point, but no one
smoked on TV anymore.
   "What?"
   "I'm almost afraid to say it."
   "Come on, you know I'm not the violent type."

This was a bit out of character because in many of the episodes he very definitely was the violent type, though he had never been violent with Cheryl, at least in the episodes I'd seen. He saved his violent impulses for his professional life.

"I'm pregnant..." Pause. A shot of Skellings' face, looking incredulous.

"You're pregnant."

"That's what I said. Please don't be mad, Ralph. It just happened."

"But you can't be pregnant. I mean ..."

"Of course I can. I am."

"Not by me, kiddo. I've had a vasectomy." He picks up the paper on his lap but quickly puts it down again. *"You'll have to think again."*

"A vasectomy! You never told me!"

"Well, it's not something a guy chats about. It was a long time ago. I knew I'd never want any kids. I knew I wasn't father material."

This was a Skellings I'd never seen before. A vasectomy! As a plot point? Were the writers getting desperate?

"And all this time I've been so careful. If I'd known I could have stopped taking those damn pills."

"Apparently not. Who've you been seeing?" He doesn't say this with anger, the script points out, just with curiosity.

She gets teary and wipes her eyes. *"I never see anyone else, really. Hardly ever. It's just that ... you've been so busy, and we haven't had much time together... I get lonely. I used to think we might have a life together, but you don't seem to ..."*

"I never promised that. With what I do for a living? You wouldn't want to live with that. I told you a long time ago I'm not the marrying kind."

I was more and more amazed, reading this. It was unlike all the other *Crime City* episodes. I'd have to rethink the way I played him. Must be a new writer not used to our old Skellings.

"*You know who it is?*"

"*Of course I know. What do you take me for? It was this guy I met in a bar a couple of months ago. We were playing pool, and when he saw how good I was, he …*"

"*You don't need to tell me. I'm not really interested.*"

A silence while Cheryl cries.

"*I only saw him that one time. Okay, maybe twice. It didn't mean anything. I was lonely, and you kept breaking dates. It was that drug case, I think. You were so involved, you could hardly concentrate on anything else.*"

He raises his voice. "*I said you don't have to tell me.*"

"*Okay, okay. But what should I do? I don't have the money. And I can't take care of a baby.*"

I realized at this point that I didn't know—we, the audience, didn't know—what Cheryl did for a living, if anything. Or more likely this had been established before my accident, before I forgot everything. With her curly blonde hair and pert nose and full lips, I could imagine her as a cigarette girl in one of those old crime movies, where girls walk through nightclubs carrying cartons of cigarettes from a strap slung around their necks and move smiling through the crowd of drinkers. But there were no cigarette girls anymore, perish the thought. Though I could be misjudging her. She could be a model, or work in a department store, the perfume department, maybe, spraying passing shoppers. A waitress? No, more likely the hostess in an upscale place, who welcomes guests, holding a batch of huge menus.

Skellings softens at this point. He strokes her cheek. "*Not to worry,*" he says. "*I'll take care of it.*"

"*Do you mean you'll give me the money?*"

"*You find the doctor, and I'll take you there and do whatever you need. I guess in other circumstances I could be the father,*" *couldn't I?"* They were skirting the boundaries of what our audience would accept. Hadn't Jonathan thought about that?

She leans over to hug him and kiss his cheek. *"Oh, thank you, Ralph. I was afraid of how you'd take it. To tell the truth I was scared to tell you. But you're a good guy, Ralphie. You are good to me."*

Ralphie! This was almost too far out to be believed. And he accepted her caresses.

"I'm sorry. I'm sorry you have to go through it. Look, I know I don't have any right to say how you should spend your free nights. Not with the way things are. But Cheryl, at least be careful."

"I will," she says humbly. *"I've hardly ever seen any other guys since we started, Ralphie, I swear. And I won't again."* Pause. *"I never ask you what you do."*

He chuckles. *"I don't do anything. I'm too mixed up with criminals."*

"I hope you're careful, Ralphie. You know I worry for you. If we lived together, it would be different ... But I know how you feel about your independence."

I suddenly had an awful suspicion that Skellings would soften up—it would take a few weeks, but this might be the start—and move in with Cheryl, or more likely have her move in with him. Her apartment looked small and cluttered, magazines scattered around, a few articles of clothing thrown over a chair, and even though we'd never seen his place, the brownstone where he turned his key in the door at the end of each episode looked solid and well-kept. It looked almost like my own building, disturbingly so. He could give up the private investigator line and go into some safer kind of work; they might even settle down and raise a family. They weren't too old. Vasectomies can be reversed.

I would be out of a job. That was the key point. I

ought to ask Jonathan if this scene was the beginning of the end for *Crime City* and my so-far dependable career. What else could I do in my present condition? Another acting job? I suppose so. It would mean interviews and auditions. I had an agent, of course, but she hadn't kept busy on my behalf lately. I must remember to call her. I hadn't been in touch since I got out of the hospital.

Fortunately, the rest of the script—this opening scene had taken longer than most, nearly ten minutes, long for TV scenes nowadays, and without a commercial break for guy products—got Skellings involved in a new case, a group of tenants wanting to sue their landlord for various violations, the worst of them involving asbestos. It would surely be carried over into the next week. I slammed the script shut. With luck Cheryl's abortion would go smoothly, and we'd hear no more about it. I still couldn't take in an abortion on *Crime City*. The sponsors wouldn't go for it. And neither did I. I wanted things to go back the way they were, with no more about intimate relations between Cheryl and Skellings. Certainly not marriage, or even living together. I didn't want to play a tamed Skellings.

HER NAME WAS EMILY. WHY DO I SAY "WAS?" Surely it's still her name, and she must be wondering why I never showed up for the coffee date we'd made for the day after my accident. Or maybe not. Maybe she didn't care, or simply forgot, but not for the same reason I did.

She was a photographer. She'd come to the studio to get some quick shots for the network's fall advertising campaign. Blonde, tall, and broad shouldered, her hair in a long braid down her back, dressed in black jeans and a loose black shirt, with a camera around her neck and a couple of young male assistants following her around. She wore large silver hoop earrings and a wide belt that ended in a V just below her waist. High-heeled black laced boots. An arty type—there'd been lots of those in grad school (vague memory or just general knowledge?). We were all hastily introduced, then she got to work. I couldn't take my eyes off her. Maybe it was her half open mouth and crooked front teeth, or her intense concentration—she seemed barely to notice us as she worked, just gave quick commands about where to stand and what to do. She had me pose with a gun in my right hand. Skellings rarely appeared with a gun, I tried to tell her, but she said that didn't matter. "It's just for publicity," she murmured. "And can you look slightly more menacing?" I tightened my face and tensed my body, which seemed to satisfy her. "Very good. I'm scared to death."

She was about my age, maybe a bit older, and she moved with an absorbed grace, as if unaware of what her body was doing. Sometimes she put a foot on a chair for a better angle; I was entranced by the right angle made by her bent leg in the tight black jeans. When the shoot was over, we all sat down at the conference table with coffee. I managed to sit next to her, and when she got up to leave, I offered to help her to the elevator with the equipment, which was elaborate. "Thanks, but no, I have my guys," and she waved to the assistants like a formidable teacher.

"I'll go down with you and point you in the right direction." I didn't want to see her go. The whole episode had a dream-like quality; something utterly new and unexpected had entered my mixed-up life, and I couldn't bear to see it vanish. I went down in the elevator, which was crowded with the four of us and their equipment, and I helped get it out to the street. They had a van parked down the block.

"Look, I'd love to see you again," I said. "I've always been fascinated by photography." I felt, and was sure I sounded, like a teenager, but I had to say something before she disappeared.

"I'll be back next week. We have to do some more, with the settings."

"Good," I said. "Then maybe we can make a date for lunch, and you can tell me how you got into this business."

She laughed; my clunky approach surely deserved to be laughed at. But she didn't say no. And when she reappeared a week later, we lingered for a while in the conference room with our coffee while the others went back to work and her assistants disappeared somewhere.

I could barely remember when I'd felt that powerfully drawn to a woman. Well, of course I couldn't remember. But I remember now. It hadn't been the same with Norah. At school, it was she who pursued me until I came to appreciate her beauty, her cleverness and competence, and how, as my mother would have said, she had my number. And when she got pregnant and wouldn't get rid of it, it seemed to me I had no choice. I went into it willingly and have had no regrets since—at least none that I recall, or allow myself to recall. Because no one like Emily had ever turned up. But this, with Emily, was like an adolescent's instant falling in love, and with someone unattainable like a movie star or rock singer. But she wasn't unattainable—she had sat beside me drinking lukewarm black coffee and munching on a brioche. Nor was she anything like the women I knew before Norah, before drama school, when I was taking odd jobs at bookstores or hauling packages at department stores wondering what to do with my life. I met those women at clubs or bars, and they were from exotic places, Egypt, Chile; they were dark and lush, and our affairs were brief. Emily was nothing like that. In fact the person she most resembled was my blonde and sturdily built high school girlfriend, Barbara, who caused one of the most mortifying moments of my life when, dancing close and slow at the graduation prom, she asked if I could move the flashlight in my pocket, it was poking at her. I prayed to die on the spot. In fact, that was the night of the auto accident that I blamed on Susan. Perhaps my embarrassment had something to do with my unforgivable betrayal.

But I'd never felt fascinated by Barbara—an ordinary neighborhood girl—as I did now: it was as if Emily came from another planet. I scrutinized everything, the way she spoke and the movements of her lips, the way she moved, that athletic build and walk, the way she handled the camera and adjusted the lights. My breath caught in my throat when I gazed at her, and it seemed my whole life before she appeared had been wasted, or at least insignificant. I forgot my work, my house, my family and indulged in graphic fantasies of being in bed with her, what I would do, what she would say, the feel of her bare skin against mine ... I was already plotting how I could manage it. All I accomplished, though, was a lunch date for the following week, at a place near the studio. I didn't want to go anywhere in my neighborhood. A lunch date I never kept.

AND SO MY MEMORY WAS COMING BACK as the pudgy bespectacled doctor predicted, and not long after that disappointing meeting with him. It came in fits and starts and wasn't all good. Remembering Emily and our missed date was embarrassing, but I had a good reason. Surely there would be worse. Now that my poor brain (I actually felt sorry for it, having gone through so much recently) is crowded with memories, mostly trivial—the map of the world hanging in my sixth-grade classroom, a game of Frisbee when I was hit hard on the shoulder, guys from high school I'd lost touch with—I don't feel quite the relief I expected. Or the gratitude. Because I will never know what parts are still missing. It's possible that what I'm missing are merely the swaths of memory that everyone forgets: after all, no one can remember everything or would even want to. There are things I would prefer to have forgotten permanently, like the pair of lovers in *Eternal Sunshine of the Spotless Mind* (although they later go on to make the same mistakes). I would like to forget the way I wangled the role of Hotspur that my classmate Nolan was far better suited for. Helped along by what Saul had told me, I remembered that all too well now, along with my feeling of triumph tainted with guilt.

Near the end of the novel about Stiller, his friend, who is also the prosecutor in his case, remarks about "the difficult step, of emerging from resigned regret that one is not what one would so much have liked to be and of becoming what one is. Nothing is harder than to accept oneself." I was coming to know that although my contempt for what I had done had come after my loss of memory. Stiller reached this stage by will alone, and rejected himself. I'm too enmeshed in my life; I'm in no position to do that. I don't even want to leave the old life behind—what would I do, and where would I go? I simply wanted to erase the parts of me that brought disgust.

I still suspect there is something significant lost forever. It might be the death of my brother Tommy at two, which my mother tried to make me forget, and succeeded. Whether this or any other missing piece would change who I feel myself to be, or who I actually am, I can't say. There is a gap in my life, or in my mind, and it waits like a pit I might someday fall into. So I proceed carefully, as if at any moment I might stumble and slip into the pit and be lost to myself again. Psychiatrists claim that everything remains somewhere, the unconscious or subconscious, though I've never totally accepted these obscure locations as a reality. Better, perhaps, to have some memories hermetically sealed, like the memory of my father's death. Indeed, much of his life. Conscious memories can be bad enough. If we sequester other memories, it's probably for a good reason.

And yet I'd like everything back, even the bad moments. To figure out whether I can respect myself or not. I still can't remember what happened with Sandra, still can't believe it really happened, even though I see the living evidence of it in Luz every day; I see how a stupid mistake can result in a great love. I can't recall the baby brother who died of meningitis. I can't recall the dreadful episode in the car that Susan told me about.

I GOT IN TOUCH WITH EMILY AND EXPLAINED why I'd never shown up for our lunch date. I didn't tell her about the amnesia, naturally—I didn't want to start out sounding like a freak—but I did say the shock to my head had erased everything from the past week. She seemed to accept that and agreed to meet for coffee in a few days. Too busy for lunch, she said.

Would we ever work up to dinner? And what else? She suggested a simple diner in midtown; obviously, she didn't have romance in mind. I made sure Vince could pick Luz up at preschool; already starting with lies …

To begin with, it felt like a first date: the facts. She was from California, had gone to UCLA, got started in photography. I tried to sound interested though I was impatient to get past the preliminaries. I offered a few facts of my own, including the Yale Drama School, to impress her.

Finally, "Look, I'd love to see you again when you're not so rushed. Maybe dinner one night?" It never occurred to me that she might be living with someone, even married.

"You're married, right? You have kids."

"Yes. How do you know that?"

"People talked about you at the studio. I'd better tell you right away, I don't get involved with married men."

"We're not involved. I'm just talking about a simple dinner."

"Oh, come off it. You know what you want it to lead to. You probably play around a lot like this. But I'm not up for it."

"I don't 'play around,' as you put it. Not at all. This is not even playing around—we're having a cup of coffee. But why do you feel that way? Are you living with some-one?"

"No. Not now. But I've been there. I had a long-distance relationship with a guy from Brazil. I met him on assignment there, in Rio. It started out great but turned into a disaster."

There followed an involved story of misunderstand-ing, resentment on both sides, a stormy parting … I didn't take the trouble to follow the details. "It took me months to recover, and I never did, quite. So just forget it." She started to reach for the jacket on the back of her chair.

"Hold on, at least finish your lunch. I'm sorry to hear that. I—I … You interest me more than any woman I've met in ages. Maybe forever."

"What about your wife?"

She doesn't count, was my immediate thought, but I checked myself before those awful words were out. She's my wife, I almost said. I love her, but … But what? This would be separate, a parallel life.

"I'd never want to hurt her."

"Just a secret fling, you mean, for as long as it interests you, and then that's it. A month, a year, until something goes wrong or one of us gets too involved?"

"I hadn't thought that far," I admitted. "I've never done this before."

"Well, take my advice, from someone who's been there. Let well enough alone. You'll be saving yourself and someone else a lot of pain."

A last-ditch effort. "Well, tell me, if I weren't married, would you be interested?"

"I might. But you are married, so there's no point in speculating."

"Will I see you around the studio? I mean, are you done with the shoot?"

"Yes. It went very well. You look great."

She got up to leave.

"Hold on, I'll go out with you." I flung some cash on the table and rushed after her. This made for an awkward parting on a noisy corner of 7th Avenue, cars, trucks, an ambulance siren wailing. I reached out to shake hands, a dumb gesture, I knew, but what else could I do? Just as she put her hand in mine, I saw a familiar girl approaching, obviously with her mother, an attractive plump woman with the same blonde hair and coloring as the girl. Before I could place her, she darted over.

"Hi, Mr. Marzino," she said enthusiastically. "It's me, Samantha. You know, Vince's girlfriend?"

The tooth fairy, right there on 7th Avenue, carrying a shopping bag from Macy's!

"Hi, Samantha. What a surprise. How are you doing?"

"This is my mom, Laura. Mom, this is Vince's dad, Mr. Marzino, the actor. You know, from *Crime City*."

The woman offered her hand. "Of course. I've watched your show. Pleased to meet you."

What would I do about Emily? Must I introduce them? I turned quickly, but Emily was gone, already a couple of feet away. She turned to give a parting nod. A relief.

"Looks like your friend is in a hurry," said Samantha's mother.

"She's in the middle of work. It was a business meeting ..." I stammered. Who was it who said, Never apologize, never explain?

I said I had to get back to the studio, and rushed off in the direction of the subway. So there was my foray into a real affair. I didn't think I'd ever done it before, but how could I be sure? (Sandra didn't count.) Judging from my lack of success, probably not. So that was over. Though I was disappointed, I knew I might have felt worse later, if it had worked out. As Stiller's friend tells him, "We can't just switch over to another life when things go wrong." Maybe that's what I'd been trying to do with Emily. "After all, it's our life that has gone wrong. Our one and only life."

How would I ever explain this to Norah, if Samantha took it into her head to say she'd run into me? I could always say I was shopping in Macy's, just as she and her mother were. Still … I was clearly not cut out for a life of deception. If meeting the Tooth Fairy casually on the street made me anxious, how would it have been if I'd met her coming out of some seedy hotel with Emily, or Emily's apartment, wherever that might be. Samantha, on the other hand, didn't seem disturbed at all. Did her mother know how many nights she'd spent in Vince's bed? Or did she say she was staying over with a girlfriend? If she lied, then we each had something on the other. I hadn't done anything except drink a cup of coffee, but already I felt the guilt of an adulterer. This was turning out to be more complicated than I'd anticipated. Maybe if I'd had a friend who was experienced in such matters …

WE HAD A QUICK REHEARSAL, AND I HEADED home, hoping for a couple of hours alone to settle my mind, but I was surprised to find Norah home early from work, upstairs in Luz's room, where Luz was crying. Norah was trying to soothe her, rubbing her stomach.

"What's the matter? Did something happen?" I immediately was horrified by the idea that Sandra had turned up at preschool again and frightened the poor kid out of her wits.

"She has a stomach ache. It started at school, they called me at work, and I rushed home. Didn't you get my text? I'm glad you're here. She's had a stomach ache now for a couple of days in a row. It's no good. We've got to get her to the Emergency Room."

I hadn't seen the text. I'd been too preoccupied to check my phone—another result of my stab at adultery. "Really? Have you tried anything else, Pepto-Bismol, that kind of stuff?"

"No, this is worse. Come on, let's not waste any more time. I was waiting for you."

She hustled us off in a cab to the ER which I remembered all too well from my visits not long ago. Luz kept crying all the way there, more like wailing, with occasional shrieks, and she clutched her stomach. I was now as alarmed as Norah—I had never heard Luz like this, at least since I'd come home from the hospital. Aside from a few crying spells over incidents in preschool, and of course the incident with Sandra, I hadn't heard her cry very often. Something else I'd have to ask Norah about. Luz seemed a remarkably calm child who took small disappointments philosophically, if one can use that term for a four-year-old. Maybe it was being the youngest and being fussed over and lovingly indulged.

She was taken in right away, and we trotted after the gurney. It didn't take the doctor long to examine her and announce, "I think it's her appendix, and we might have to operate right away."

Operate! The word scared me shitless, Norah too. We glanced at each other and gasped. Luz was quieter and half asleep—the doctor had given her something to calm her. The screams had been easier to bear than the dead silence. It wasn't long before she was whisked away—we barely had a moment to kiss her and say we'd see her soon. "We'll be in touch as soon as we can," the doctor told us. "I'm not the surgeon on duty, but I've arranged everything, and it shouldn't be long before she gets ready. You can come upstairs to wait until it's over. The doctor will come out and find you." With that she dashed away.

I was more familiar with this vast hospital than I would have liked. Before my accident, there'd been the visit with Vince—now a clear memory—when I'd had to wait far longer than this time. Not an emergency. And no doubt several other trips I didn't remember. It was good to have forgotten those. Maybe there should be some kind of folder or bin in the mind where one could put unpleasant but ultimately insignificant memories; in fact there probably already was something of the sort. Not what they call the unconscious—that was for important things.

In the waiting room, Norah and I settled in to worry on a pink plastic couch next to a candy machine. I remembered when there'd been cigarette machines all over, though perhaps not in hospitals. I gazed around at our fellow worriers, about half a dozen of them, all apparently alone except an old shabbily-dressed couple who looked grim and didn't speak to each other. One middle-aged man in jogging shorts was doing a crossword puzzle; two women were busy on their phones, and a blonde thirty-ish woman was knitting a very long narrow green scarf with a complicated design of diamond shapes that fell over her knees. It was very ugly, and I wondered who it was for. She reminded me of Emily, and I was immediately pierced by guilt, a kind of stab in the stomach, even though our meeting had come to nothing. The guilt was in the intention.

"Would you like a coffee? I could bring one from the cafeteria in the basement."

"No, I couldn't swallow anything," Norah said.

"I wish I could have a cigarette. There's a balcony somewhere on this floor."

"Joe, this is a hospital, for Chrissakes."

"Maybe I'll just dash outside for a few minutes."

"Don't leave me, please."

"All right."

In between worrying about Luz I thought about

Skellings and Cheryl's pregnancy. The latest episode had ignored it—Skellings was busy investigating the landlord who hadn't complied with the latest regulations about removing asbestos, which gave the show a chance to earn credit with environmentalists. But the theme had to recur. Something would have to interfere with the abortion he had offered to pay for. Then Skellings would marry her and settle down to some regular dull work, and I'd be out of a job.

After a long silence, Norah said, "Do you think we should let Sandra know, about the surgery, I mean? Like, just in case, God forbid, if anything happens …"

"That is about the worst idea you've ever had, that I can remember, that is. No, we should not let Sandra know. First, nothing is going to happen. It's a routine operation, the doctor probably does it every day. But more important, I don't want to ever have her in our lives again. She's caused enough trouble. And Luz is afraid of her."

"Okay," Norah answered. "I guess you're right. I was just thinking …"

"Well, don't think. She's back in California, isn't she? So let's just hope she stays there permanently."

After that I must have dozed. I woke with a start to see Norah leaping up to meet the doctor at the entrance, then grasping her hands and bursting into tears of relief. I could tell they were relief; if anything had gone wrong she'd be wailing as Luz did in the cab.

We waited until Luz was wide awake—that didn't take long—and eager to boast about her operation. She'd been very brave, the young nurse, whose tag read "Evelyn," reported, who looked scarcely older than Samantha.

Luz was too drugged to say much. But she protested

when I started to leave. "Why can't you stay with me?"

"Because you have to sleep for a while. Mommy will be here with you, and Evelyn will take good care of you. You've been so brave! But now I have to go home, and I'll see you first thing in the morning."

But the events of this dramatic day were not over yet. The boys were waiting for me in the living room—we'd already called with the good news, so I was surprised to see them still downstairs so late.

"Grandma called," Kevin announced, with an air of importance. "Your grandma died." He seemed proud to have important news. "She was ninety-three."

I collapsed on the sofa. Once again I had neglected to check my phone where I found a text from my mother with the news and information about the funeral, which would take place in two days.

I can't say I was deeply grieved. I wanted to be grieved; I wanted the stories and songs I'd loved to come back, dragging my childhood along with them, but all I recalled of her was that visit last week to the nursing home.

The only thing I wanted at that point was for nothing else to happen, but the phone rang insistently.

"You should answer," Vince said. "It might be the hospital."

"She was fine when I left." But I answered anyway.

"Joe, this is Carla. How've you been?"

"Oh, just fine. And you?"

"I have some good news. Two things, actually. I'm going to put a check in the mail to you for a thousand dollars. Not much, but it's a start. I managed to scrape it together, and I'm getting some more part-time work."

"Thanks, Carla, but really, there's no rush. You don't have to feel pressured."

"I know, but I wanted to get a start on it. The other good news is that George has signed up for Gamblers Anonymous. I finally convinced him, or maybe it was a friend he made at the track. He's promised he's finished with all that. That last threat really scared the shit out of him."

"I'm glad to hear it. Listen, I've got to go. We've had a hectic day, Luz had an emergency appendectomy, and I'm just back from the hospital. She's fine, but I'm totally wasted."

"Oh, the poor thing. I'm so glad she's okay. Keep me posted, all right?"

"Sure, and thanks again."

"I'm the one who's grateful. I think he was really in danger."

"He's more valuable alive than dead. Okay, take care."

Now please let this day be over, I prayed. I ought to call my mother, but that could wait a couple of hours. Vince ordered a pizza, and we ate it hungrily.

WHEN I PICKED UP THE LATEST SCRIPT at work, I was vastly relieved to see that Cheryl had had a miscarriage. I might have foreseen that. She called Skellings, and he dashed over and took her to the hospital. She recovered, and he was free to return to his investigating the derelict landlord. My life had changed too, in another way, and I was now able to start running again, on my healed ankle. The doctor warned me to take it easy, just half a mile or so to begin with, though I exceeded that—it felt so good to be out in the park again and moving around, on the loop with the other runners, getting glimpses of a baseball game, of the inline skaters doing their extraordinary tricks, and a group of djembe drummers pounding out a hypnotic rhythm. How could I have gone so long and not missed that?

I even went out for a short run the morning of Nonna's funeral. Luz was home, and we left the boys with her. She was up and moving around, but I wished there were a girl or woman to keep an eye on her. Not that I couldn't trust the boys, but I'd feel more comfortable with a female presence. I even asked Vince if Samantha might come over.

"We broke up," he said curtly.

"When was this?"

"The day you took Luz to the hospital."

"Any special reason?"

"Well," he looked slightly sheepish, "I met someone else. Another girl at school."

"Samantha must have been hurt," I put in.

"She took it better than I expected. I have an idea she's interested in another guy, someone from the football team."

"And who is the new girl?"

"She's great. I'll invite her over soon. She's from Senegal. Her French is perfect, well, that's her first language. But she's been here for a few years, so her English is very good too. Her father does something in electronics."

We could invite her over with Clara and Ken from upstairs, I thought, but of course didn't say. How long would it be before she was wandering around upstairs in the middle of the night in a shortie nightgown? Would Luz be surprised, or worse, disillusioned to see a different tooth fairy? I'd always pictured the tooth fairy as white, but that was undoubtedly a prejudice. Why shouldn't the tooth fairy be Black? Surely in Senegal she was. I'd miss

Samantha, whom I'd gotten accustomed to as a frequent guest and who had proved useful around the house, loading the dishwasher and lugging out the garbage. On the other hand there was now no danger of her mentioning meeting me down on 7th Avenue as I was taking leave of Emily. Or Emily taking leave of me, I should say.

"Well, good. What's her name?"

"Amina. Isn't that a nice name?"

IN THE END, SANDRA'S AUNT WAS ENLISTED to stay with Luz while we all attended Nonna's funeral. I hadn't expected the boys to come since they'd rarely seen her, but they were curious about funerals: this would be their first.

It was a small affair, our family, Susan, one or two friends from the senior living home, and a couple of old women I didn't recognize. I stayed close to my mother, who shed a few tears but otherwise was her usual resilient self. On the way out she took my arm—she was tottering on the wet grass in her elegant high black boots, laced to the knee. I was wearing a pair of old and fairly shabby shoes.

"I knew it would rain," she said. "It always rains at funerals."

In fact it had been a rainy couple of weeks, relieved by a few patches of brilliant sunshine. "Oh, does it?" I asked. I couldn't remember any. I must have attended my father's, though my recalcitrant memory refused to yield it up.

Before we got into the waiting cars, my mother said, "Just a moment, there's something I need to tell you."

Nothing bad, I pleaded within. There had been too

many changes in too short a time. Was this what ordinary life was like for people with unblemished memories? Now that I could remember so much more, it seemed the past few days had been packed with more events than usual.

She cleared her throat before she began. "I know you and Susan have always been puzzled about your father's death. The little you know, I think, gives the impression that he was involved with well, what you'd call shady characters ..."

"Well, wasn't he?"

"Only in a sense. He was ... he was helping the police, or the FBI, or whoever does those things."

"An informer?" Visions of crime episodes I'd seen on TV and in films came flooding into my head. And over all the images loomed the face and figure of Skellings, which were of course my own. This was entirely too weird.

"If that's what they call people who do that. You must know more about it than I do—" she gave a curt laugh—"given your life of crime, your TV life."

"I know nothing about it. I only say the lines they give me in the script."

"He was doing dangerous and important work," she said huffily.

"Dangerous enough to get himself killed, it seems. Didn't he know how to protect himself? How do people get into that line of work anyway?"

"I wouldn't know. That's the kind of thing you should have asked Nonna when she was alive. I think it was after his death that she started to go downhill."

Car horns were honking. We were holding up the funeral procession, cars eager to leave. "Did she really know about it?"

"I don't know how much she knew. I knew very little —he thought I'd be safer that way. He'd rather you and Susan suspected him of minor crimes than of being an informer."

So even the little I knew and remembered was false. How could I trust any memories, or memory at all?

"How did you live with that?"

"He kept me in the dark, I told you. He feared for my safety, and as soon as he was gone, I moved away, as you know."

"A strange way to live, wasn't it?" I asked. "Not knowing really what your husband was doing and how endangered he was?"

She was silent for a moment while the horns blared, then took my arm and started walking towards the waiting cars. "A lot of people live without knowing much about the truth of their lives." With that sphinxlike remark she walked faster and hustled off to join the others, then turned back. "You should know something about that."

I TRUST NOW THAT THE REST OF MY LIFE will return, or most of it. So says the marble-eyed doctor, and I believe him. I await these unexpected and disorganized intrusions of memory with eagerness and dread. Could they be worse than what I've already recovered? Or most likely more of the same. If I know the worst, the rest can't help but be better. Happy memories in which I'm, if not a terrific guy, at least someone I can live with, as I'm striving to learn to live with what I've already discovered.

Norah is delighted with my "improvement."

"You'll be the man you were. He wasn't so bad, all things considered," and she laughs with relief and throws her arms around me.

I won't be the man I was. I awoke from the accident without a past, innocent as a newborn, well, almost. I'll never forget those weeks when I was flailing around, trying to learn who I was, not knowing what to do with each fact and act I stumbled on. Where to fit them. That flailing man was someone else, in his innocence and confusion. I almost miss him. He was not easy to be—or to portray—in his ignorance and plain stupidity. But he was sincere and tried to behave well. I'll miss that. His awkward efforts to do the right thing. I'll be having to live with a more sophisticated man, one whose efforts are constrained by all sorts of subtle considerations and a wealth of self-knowledge. *Know thyself,* ancient wisdom tells us. And I will, and I will know how arduous a process that is.

Kevin was chosen to play the clarinet part in the school's final orchestra performance, to no one's surprise. He reported this to us with a gleeful enthusiasm I hadn't seen in him before, or so I thought at the time. Amina is now a frequent overnight guest, as cooperative and amiable as her predecessor, Samantha, and has never been found in the hall late at night. Luz is the same; she wants a guinea pig, which I suppose we can learn to accommodate. My mother has a boyfriend, a man about her age who came into the store looking for a tuxedo for a wedding. He's an accountant at a large firm, nothing shady about him that we can discern, so we're happy for her. Susan is back in Colorado. She, or I should say we, were successful in persuading the Cooper Hewitt Museum to take two pieces of Monica's pottery, unusual bowls resembling small animals.

Monica would deal with the financial aspects, Susan said—we were only the delivery staff. And Norah, to the best of my knowledge, is still posing at the Art Students League. She comes home late two nights a week, and I prepare dinner, and we say no more about it. Nor about divorce. I still can't remember what prompted me to suggest it before my accident. I suppose I'll remember at some point, but by then it shall be ancient history. If I was having an affair, which I doubt, no one has come forward to remind me.

I offer these details partly to reassure myself that my life has its narrative and characters who appear and reappear and play their assigned roles as in ordinary lives. The same goes for Skellings: he persists in his tough-guy-with-a-soft-heart role as usual, never being outwitted for long. I'm fortunate: he's an easy role to play, and I hope he continues into the unforeseeable future.

LYNNE SHARON SCHWARTZ is the author of thirty books of fiction, essays, and poetry, including her novels *Leaving Brooklyn*, a finalist for the PEN/Faulkner Award, and *Rough Strife*, a finalist for the National Book Award. She has also published two memoirs, *Ruined by Reading* and *Not Now, Voyager*, and has translated from the Italian. Schwartz has been the recipient of fellowships from the Guggenheim Foundation, the National Endowment for the Arts in Fiction and, separately, for Translation, and the New York State Foundation for the Arts. She has taught widely, most recently at the Bennington College Writing Seminars and the Columbia University School of Arts.